Mills & Boon

BEST SELLER ROMANCE

A chance to read and collect some of the best-loved novels from Mills & Boon—the world's largest publisher of romantic fiction.

Every month, three titles by favourite Mills & Boon authors will be re-published in the *Best Seller Romance* series.

A list of other titles in the *Best Seller Romance* series can be found at the end of this book.

Mary Wibberley

RUNAWAY MARRIAGE

MILLS & BOON LIMITED
15–16 BROOK'S MEWS
LONDON W1A 1DR

First published in Great Britain 1979
by Mills & Boon Limited

© Mary Wibberley 1979

Australian copyright 1979
Philippine copyright 1979
Reprinted 1979
This edition 1985

ISBN 0 263 75313 1

Set in Linotype Plantin 11 on 13 pt.
02–1185

Made and printed in Great Britain by
Richard Clay (The Chaucer Press) Ltd,
Bungay, Suffolk

CHAPTER ONE

IT was the last straw. It was absolutely and positively the last straw. Very calmly and deliberately, Jan Hunter tore the two engraved invitation cards into little pieces and let them flutter to the floor. Then she picked up the pad that was by the telephone, turned over the top page, the one with her mother's note on, and began to write.

Five minutes later she slammed out of the front door of the elegant house in St John's Wood, flung her hastily packed suitcase in the back seat of her red Jaguar and drove away, scattering gravel in all directions as she skidded out of the gate. Behind her, at an upstairs window, the lace curtain fluttered, and the housekeeper shook her head and gave a little sigh. She'd been expecting this for weeks. She wondered what Mrs Hunter would have to say when she came home at lunch. It was nothing she cared to dwell on.

Jan drove out of London as if she were pursued. Damn them all, damn the wedding, damn Jeremy. . . . She switched on the radio, because she didn't want to have to think about them at all. She wanted to get away—and she was going to. She was going to escape to the one true haven she had: her Aunt Jessie's cottage in Cornwall. She would understand, and she alone. Jan ached to pour her heart out to her, to tell her how, with the wedding only one week away, the pressure had built up so that it was too much to bear any more. She should have gone weeks ago.

The wedding had been going to be a quiet one, at first. Jeremy thought it a splendid idea. He hated fuss as much as Jan—or so it had seemed. But then her mother had taken over, and subtly, oh, so very subtly, everything had changed—including Jeremy. It had all happened gradually. There had been no point at which she could have said: 'Whoa, that's enough!' because it was so careful, so casual, this transition from local church, reception at home with just a few close relatives and friends to a three hundred guest affair at the Hilton, and of course with *that* many the church round the corner wouldn't be good enough.... Subtle, very subtle the process of erosion. And she, dazzled by everything, too happy with her darling Jeremy to care, had allowed herself to be swept along with it all.

She shivered and turned on the heater, although it was a warm summer's day. She couldn't tell anyone about the sudden feelings of panic, because they would all laugh, and say knowingly that it was pre-wedding nerves, and it would be all right on the night, nudge nudge. She knew her friends, and Jeremy's friends— and her mother's. But this, just now, this morning, had been the last straw. Her mother's note had been precise and economical, as always. It had told Jan to write those two invitations—last-minute, of course, to two dear friends who were coming over from America on business. Simple enough, but on top of what had happened the previous night, when she had had the row with Jeremy, too much.

She turned off the radio, too hurt to listen any more to the inane chatter of a disc jockey. Jeremy had hurt her because he genuinely didn't understand why she had asked if they couldn't just cancel the grand honeymoon in the Bahamas and go to his cottage in the Lakes. His expression had been one of amazement as he said: 'But darling, we're going to have a fabulous fortnight. The Fitzgeralds are giving us a bungalow on the beach, and they'll keep well out of the way, you know that.'

'But they've organised parties and barbecues and heaven knows what. I just want to be alone with *you*— don't you see?'

'Of course I do, my precious, and God knows, I can't *wait*—but they're friends of Dad's. What on earth will they think if we cancel?'

She had screamed something at him then, to the effect that she didn't care what his father, or his father's friends, or her mother, or her mother's friends thought, and he'd gone off in a huff, with the crushing remarks that lingered long afterwards that she didn't know what she was saying, she would soon be part of his world, and she'd better get used to the idea, that she was far too snappy just lately, and that as the wife of the heir to the Redmayne fortune she ought to be jolly well appreciative of everything.

Money. It was all her mother ever thought about, and it was all Jeremy ever thought about. And between the two of them, they were taking over her life. She knew she could change him when they were married,

knew she could make him see there were other things
in life more important. But not yet, not while he and
his father and her mother were so busy organising
everything between them.

Let them. She would sit and toast her toes by Aunt
Jessie's fire, and drink hot cocoa, while they wrote out
their own last-minute invitations and saw that the
flowers were the most expensive in London. They
would manage very well—probably better—without
her. Then she would go back home on the Friday with
Aunt Jessie, and she and Jeremy would marry and live
happily ever after—with any luck.

Her mouth was dry. She hadn't eaten since the
previous afternoon, and although her stomach was
empty she couldn't eat a thing. But she needed a drink.
She stopped in a little village and had a cup of coffee,
then bought some groceries to take to her aunt's. Two
hours later she was bumping up the final stretch of
track, the sea to her left, crashing against the rocks, the
windswept trees and bushes to her right. Only another
mile.... Then she saw a house, half built, and slowed
down. Another house, *here*? A lorry was parked outside, and a cement mixer stood like a fat grey sentry in
front, but there were no signs of life. Jan frowned. She
had never imagined anyone would want to build just
here, beautiful though it was, but the land belonged to
her aunt, and surely, if she had sold some, they would
have known about it? She would soon be there, and
London, and the wedding, had receded with the miles,
and no longer seemed so important.

She gave a little sigh of relief as the cottage came in sight, and slowed the Jaguar to a crawl because the road surface was appalling, and ruinous to tyres. How her aunt drove that Mini Jan had never been able to imagine. She smiled to herself at the thought.

She walked towards the door, pushed it open, and called: 'Aunt Jessie, it's me!' The two Irish wolf-hounds bounded out, nearly knocking her over in the enthusiasm of their welcome, and she put the box of groceries down on the bench and laughed. 'Hello Domino, Finn, where's your——'

She stopped. A man stood in the doorway to the kitchen, shadowed, because she was still blinking from the sun, and stood in the light, but she could see from there that he was big and tough-looking, and very dark. Then he spoke.

'Hello,' he said. 'Who are you?' Two things registered. He spoke with a decidedly foreign accent— and his voice held no welcome at all. Jan straightened from patting the huge dogs and then walked slowly towards him, the better to see him. The hair prickled on the back of her neck in sudden irrational fear. What was he doing here? Yet the dogs were not afraid—or bothered.

'Who are *you*?' she demanded. 'This is my aunt's house, and——'

'I know whose house it is. I don't know you.' Not rude, not quite, but arrogant. His voice was deep, and he spoke quietly, but with a force she found disturbing. Her nerve ends were too ragged after all that had happened for her to speak normally.

'My name is Jan Hunter,' she snapped. 'My Aunt Jessie owns this house. Where is she?'

He turned away without a word and walked back into the kitchen to switch off the kettle that had begun to whistle. Jan followed him in. There she saw him clearly for the first time, and that was even more disturbing. He was tall and broad-shouldered. That much she had already seen, but not the details that completed the picture. Now she looked at him, and her heart bumped in sudden dismay—and fear. He looked like a gipsy, dressed in tattered jeans and checked shirt with the sleeves rolled up to the elbows to reveal very muscular strong-looking arms.

His face was riveting. There was no other way to describe it, because she couldn't, for the moment, take her eyes away from it. Tanned and hard-looking, with deep-set grey eyes. Slightly broad nose—as though it had been broken at some time—wide mouth and tough chin, he looked as though he would have been more at home on a fishing boat than in a civilised, tidy kitchen. His hair was jet black, and short, and he had the neck of a rugby player, a thick strong neck. He looked at her now and said : 'Do you think you will know me next time you see me?'

She flushed, and felt stupid for having done so. She did not like him. He smiled, as if amused at her discomfiture. 'My name is Sandor Gregas, and I am staying here as your aunt's guest,' he said quietly, 'and I am about to make myself a cup of coffee. Would you like one?'

She was tempted to tell him what to do with his cup of coffee, but resisted the temptation, with difficulty. Her reaction to him was so strong that it disturbed her. But he was Aunt Jessie's guest....

'Please.' She sat down. 'Is my aunt out?'

He was busy pouring the water into a percolator and didn't answer immediately. Then he turned. 'I prefer ground coffee. I hope you do.' He said it as though it didn't matter anyway, she could take it or leave it. 'Your aunt is not here.'

'I can see that,' she answered.

'I mean she is away. In London.'

The words fell like ice into the warm room. 'Oh no!' she burst out. 'In *London*? But I've just come from there——' her eyes were wide with dismay.

He shrugged. 'That is unfortunate. She said nothing about you——'

'She didn't know I was coming——' Jan stopped. She had no intention of telling him anything about herself.

'Perhaps that is why she said nothing.' He produced two clean beakers from the draining board and put them on the table.

'But why has she left *you* here?' she demanded.

He raised one thick black eyebrow. 'Why? Why should she not? Someone has to feed the dogs.' Domino and Finn, leaning heavily against Jan's legs, wagged their long tails slowly as if they knew he was talking about them, and looked at him. She drew in her breath.

'I didn't mean that,' she countered, feeling on the defensive. She wasn't strong enough to take much more from this hard, arrogant man, not after all that had happened, and he seemed to be enjoying himself, which made it worse. What made it even worse was the fact that Aunt Jessie wasn't in the habit of entertaining strange men, and particularly dark gipsyish tough-looking men who seemed totally out of place in that small cottage. His presence filled the kitchen with a force and power that were eminently disturbing.

'What did you mean?' He poured out the coffee and put a milk bottle on the table.

'She doesn't usually have visitors,' she said. 'How do I know——'

'That I am not a burglar?' he cut in. 'You don't. You will have to take my word for it—or telephone your aunt. She is staying in London at a friend's and has left her number by the phone.' He sat opposite her at the table and gazed at her. His eyes were mesmeric. They seemed to reach into her mind. . . . She looked away. 'She has gone to this friend's because she needs to do some shopping for a wedding she is attending next week. Her niece's wedding.' Slowly, compelled by something she didn't understand, Jan looked at him. 'Is it *your* wedding she was talking about?'

'I—yes,' she whispered.

'How odd. Why have you run away?' She froze in alarm, opened her mouth to give him the pasting he deserved—and the telephone rang. Her hand jerked on the beaker, nearly knocking it over. He stood up.

'Wait——' she said desperately. 'Don't——' She ran her tongue over her dry lips.

'It is for you?' He paused by the chair.

'I think it will be.' She was white. It would be her mother; she would have read the note by now. She wasn't prepared to speak to her yet, but how could she tell him? 'I don't—want to—to——'

He sat down again. 'Then let it ring. But if it starts again, I should answer it, you know. It might not be for you.'

'Yes, I know.' It continued shrilling, as if the caller knew there was someone there, and was going to keep on and on and on. . . .

Then, mercifully, it stopped, and Jan felt herself slump in relief. She finished the coffee, which was strong, and just what she needed. 'If I am to answer it, had you not better tell me what I should say?' he asked.

'It will be my mother. She'll want to know what the hell I'm doing here,' said Jan.

'She does not already know?'

'No.'

'I see.' His mouth twitched at the corner, as if he was debating whether or not to smile.

'You don't see at all. And I don't wish to discuss it,' she snapped.

The smile that might not have been a smile vanished. His eyes narrowed. 'Then I suggest you answer the telephone yourself when it rings. You are rude enough to deal with anyone, even your own mother——'

'How dare you! How dare you be so arrogant!' she exclaimed, temper flaring.

'It is you who are arrogant,' he retorted smoothly. 'You arrive demanding to know who I am as if you are in charge of your aunt's life—and you are not. She is perfectly capable of inviting whomsoever she wants to stay, when she wants. It might be as well to remember that.'

Jan stared at him, speechless. Then she found her voice. 'You're insufferable!' she breathed.

'And you are spoilt. You need a damned good spanking!' he sparked back. She stood up.

'I'm going to telephone my aunt now. When I tell her——' She stopped, senses tingling at what she saw in those dark grey eyes.

'When you tell her what?' He rose too. 'That you don't like me? That you wish me to go? What do you think she will say?' He laughed. 'Do you think you know her that well? Do you think she will say—send him away? Go and make your phone call.'

'I'm not staying here with you!' she retorted.

'I'm sure there are hotels nearby that will accommodate you,' he said, and smiled. Jan turned and went out, trembling with impotent anger. He was hateful! She took a few deep breaths before picking up the telephone. She wasn't prepared to admit even to herself that she wanted to know exactly who he was, and what he was doing there.

Aunt Jessie was never surprised, never dismayed at

anything. Her reaction now to Jan's call was totally expected. 'Oh hello, dear,' she said, 'what a shame we missed each other! I'm up here with Dolly doing some shopping for your wedding. Still, have a nice rest while you're there——'

'But who's *he*?' Jan whispered. She had closed the door to the kitchen, but it wouldn't surprise her to think he was standing with his ear pressed against the door.

'Oh, Sandor, you mean! Gracious, I'd forgotten! Dear me,' Aunt Jessie laughed, and Jan sighed a little sigh. 'He's looking after the dogs, of course. He'll be out most of the time anyway—give him my love and tell him there's a carton of dog food in the pantry——'

'What's he *doing* here?' hissed Jan, clutching the telephone tightly.

'Oh, didn't he tell you? He's rather nice, isn't he? So lovely to have him as a neighbour——' Jan screamed silently, inwardly. 'Just ask him dear, I must go. Dolly's waving frantically at me because the taxi's waiting——' her voice came faintly, as though she had turned away—'won't be a second dear, it's Jan——' then to Jan: 'Any message for your mother, dear, if I see her?'

'No, I'll phone her. 'Bye, love, have a nice shopping trip.' Jan hung up and walked slowly back towards the kitchen. She regretted her childish outburst of temper before. Normally as calm and unruffled as her aunt, Jan's nerves, due to the intolerable pressures of a domineering mother trying to organise her wedding to suit herself, had become ragged and raw. She was scarcely aware of it herself, only of the weariness that overcame her frequently—as it had now.

She went into the kitchen, sat down, and burst into tears. As she fumbled in her handbag for a handkerchief it fell to the floor, scattering the contents widely. The dogs sniffed with interest, and Sandor Gregas knelt and gathered up the make-up, perfume, purse and wallet and put them back in. He handed her something. 'Is that what you wanted?' he said.

She took the handkerchief. 'Yes, thank you.'

He put the handbag on the table. 'Hadn't you better tell me what's wrong?' he asked her.

'Nothing's wrong—thank you for picking up my bag.' She wiped her eyes. 'You must forgive me for that silly display of tears——'

'It is not for me to forgive,' he remarked. There was a softening in him, nothing tangible, yet she sensed a lessening of his hostility. It was enough, for the moment. 'Are you staying here?'

'I have nowhere to go. There are no hotels for miles —and anyway, I didn't bring enough money—I left home in rather a hurry.' She looked at him, composure regained. 'You were right, in a way I was running away.'

'But you can hardly stay.'

'I'm not going back to London!'

'Ah.' It held a wealth of meaning. 'Then a hotel?'

'I'll have to stay here. I've no money. Only enough for petrol—I thought—I packed in a hurry——'

'With me?'

'Unless you're going to leave.'

'I too have nowhere to go. Not until I have finished building the house.'

Then she remembered. She looked at him. 'Are you working on that new house back down the road?'

'Yes. Not alone. But the other men are living in the village ten miles away——' Jan stared, aghast. How on earth had her aunt come to take him in as a lodger? He was rough, tough-looking, a foreigner, aggressive, abrasive, and a bricklayer. He must have told a good tale to her. Something must have shown in her face. She saw his expression alter subtly, and he added: 'I promise you, I won't touch her silver.'

She felt herself flush. She had been right about those eyes; they looked into her mind. Apparently they didn't like what they saw.

'I didn't say you would,' she retorted.

'But your face said it for you. Are you a snob, as well as being spoilt? A poor workman may be as honest as you are, Miss Hunter—if you are honest, that is. You seem to have left a few lies behind you——'

'What do you mean?' she snapped.

'By your reluctance to speak to your mother——'

'That doesn't mean I told lies! Don't be absurd!'

'It is you who are absurd. People don't run away if they have any guts. They stay and face the situation that bothers them, and in that way they sort it out——'

'You know nothing.' She glared at him. Let him meet her mother, he'd be different then. She'd wipe the floor with him. No, she took that back. She wouldn't wish her mother's ire on her worst enemy—and he was nobody at all. How facile his solutions! Stay and face the situation—he could have no idea of the pressures she was under. 'And I don't intend to tell you. We're stuck with each other, Mr Gregas, for the time being. Perhaps we ought to call a truce.'

'I was not aware there had been a war.' He nodded. 'However, you have a point. It is Friday, we have the weekend ahead, when there is little work done on the house, and it would be as well to live in harmony, as we are sharing the same cottage. After Monday you will have the place to yourself during the day. For how long do you intend to stay?'

She swallowed. 'I'll have to go back next week some time——'

'Indeed. Certainly for Saturday. That is your wedding day, is it not?'

'Yes.'

'Does your fiancé know you are here?'

'Only if my mother's let him know.'

'Ah, I see. You quarrelled?'

'I wish you'd stop saying "ah" and "I see"! We had a slight—disagreement, yes—not that it's any of your business——'

'Does he love you?' His impertinence took her breath away, yet somehow she was compelled to answer.

'Of course!'

'And do you love him?'

She stared had at him. 'I really don't see——'

'Please answer.'

'Of course I do.'

He nodded. 'Then telephone him. Tell him where you are.'

'Why?'

'Because he should know.' Jan looked down at her hands on the table. He was right. In a strange way he was right—but she knew she didn't want to phone Jeremy at all. She didn't want to speak to him.

CHAPTER TWO

'No,' she said. 'Not yet.' She looked up. 'I'll go and get my case from the car—I brought some food as well. The grocery van only calls once a week.'

'I know. I have been here for five weeks now.' That was a surprise. Jan had telephoned her aunt several times, and Jessie had never mentioned the strange workman lodging there. In an odd way, Jan found that hurtful. She and her aunt were so close, and yet. . . .

'I will bring in your case for you. Come.' He indicated with his hand that she was to rise, and Jan did so.

'I can manage,' she answered with dignity.

'Of course you can. Nevertheless, it would not be mannerly of me to watch you carrying your luggage in, would it?'

She had to smile at that. Manners? He had already told her she was spoilt, needed a spanking, as good as accused her of being a coward—and he talked about manners! Yet the impulse to retort was stifled. He clearly had no intention of moving out for her, and she had nowhere to go, so a modicum of tact was called for. 'Thank you,' she said, and walked out, followed by the dogs, and then Sandor Gregas.

He opened the car door and reached in for her case. 'Is this all?'

'Yes.' She slammed the door shut.

'You have a nice car. Yours?'

'Yes. A present from my mother on my twenty-first birthday.' He raised his eyebrows but made no comment, leading the way in and hefting the box of groceries from the bench by the front door as he went in. Jan followed and closed the front door after them. He put her case down in the hall and took the box through to the kitchen.

'Which room are you sleeping in?' She followed him through.

'The small boxroom at the front.' That was the one she usually slept in.

'I'll take my aunt's room. I think I'll go up and have a wash now. I'll put the food away after.'

'If the telephone rings while you are away, shall I answer?'

She hesitated. Then: 'Yes. If it's for me, say I'll ring back.'

'Very well.' He nodded as if to dismiss her.

She decided to have a bath instead of a wash, and emerged pink and glowing some twenty minutes later from the bathroom to hear him speaking on the telephone in the hall. She paused on the landing, heart thudding. She should go down, but she waited instead. Two things were clear immediately: the person he was talking to was her mother—and he was amused. The two things definitely didn't go together. She crept down and sat half way up the staircase, peeping through the banister rails, seeing him standing there, back to her, talking. He was as yet unaware of her presence.

'—I am living here,' he was saying, 'and no, I don't choose to give my reasons on the phone. I have already told you my name, madam, you have not told me yours, and if you don't speak more calmly I shall hang up on you——' She could almost hear the line explode. The next moment he put the telephone down.

She gasped, he looked up at her and smiled. It was not a pleasant smile.

'Was that your mother?' he asked.

'It sounded like it from here.' She pulled a face.

'Then you must forgive me if I was rude to her——'

'Why? She's not used to people answering her back. I'm sorry you had to listen.'

'I didn't. I hung up.' He looked at his watch. 'I estimate that she will call again in a few minutes. Do you wish to answer, or shall I?'

'I'd better, thanks.' He shrugged.

'As you wish. I must warn you, she's not pleased.'

'I gathered that.' Jan came down the last few steps. 'I don't care any more.' But she did. She felt sick inside. It had seemed such a grand gesture, packing, and storming out. 'I think I'll have a coffee before it rings again.'

'Have you eaten today?'

'No, I'm not hungry.'

'You must have something. I shall make you an omelette, I haven't eaten either, since breakfast, and I *am* hungry.'

The telephone began to ring. She looked at him, saw the expression on his face as he walked away, and picked the telephone up.

'Jan?' her mother's voice nearly shattered her eardrum. 'At *last*! My God, you'd better have a good story to tell! You've caused chaos this end—I've had Jeremy on the phone and I've had to tell him you've just up and gone—what the *hell* do you think you're playing at? And who is that abominably rude foreign peasant who answered the phone?'

'He's living here, and I've just had enough of everything—don't worry, I'll be back next week, I just need a few days to——'

'You'll be back today, you stupid little fool! Have you *forgotten* where we're all going tonight? My God, have you actually *forgotten*?' Her mother's voice rose, shrill with temper.

Jan didn't know what she was talking about. 'What?' she said, dazed.

'The reception at the Embassy? My God, I don't believe it!'

'Oh.'

'Now you get back here at once. If you drive fast you'll be home at seven—are you listening?'

'No.' The silence that followed was nearly as shattering as her mother's voice.

'What do you mean—no?'

'I'm not coming back now. I don't feel up to driving back.'

'Then get a taxi. This is a most important occasion —the Ambassador and his wife are expecting to meet you and Jeremy——'

'I can't. I've had enough.'

'Enough? Enough of what, for God's sake? You're getting married next week, or have you forgotten *that* as well?' The icicles dripped down the line. 'And if you think you're living in a cottage with some Bulgarian or heaven knows what he is, you're very mistaken, my dear. Jess's not there, is she? Just imagine if the papers get hold of that bit of information! You're so *stupid*, Jan—you always have been, but I'm not going to stand this. Now you get yourself on the phone and book a taxi——'

'No. I'm staying here.' And Jan hung up. She walked, white-faced and trembling, into the kitchen. 'Are you Bulgarian?' she asked.

'No, Hungarian. Why?'

She shook her head. 'My—my mother thought you were——' She tried to laugh but failed dismally.

'Sit down. The omelette is nearly ready.'

'Yes.' She sat down and Domino nuzzled her hand, as if sensing her unhappiness and wanting to share it. 'I hung up on her. What shall I do?'

'What do you want to do?'

'Nothing. Absolutely nothing. She wants me to go back—some do at the American Embassy I'd completely forgotten about. It's very important to her.'

'Why?'

'Because she's the director of an Anglo–American soft drink company—you've heard of Zesty-Cola?'

'I've heard of it.'

'That's my mother. She *is* Zesty-Cola.'

'Is she American?'

'No, but her third husband was, my stepfather. She's a very busy lady.'

'I'm sure. Do you want to go to this thing at the Embassy?'

'No. She uses me as decoration——' Jan stopped, horrified. Words were coming out that she had no intention of telling anyone, especially not him. 'I mean'—she had to swallow—'she likes me to go with her——'

'You are beautiful,' he said, but his eyes upon her were not that of a man smitten by her looks, more a disinterested observer weighing up a piece of art. 'But then you already know that, don't you?'

She laughed without humour. 'I'm not. Not inside. It's all top show——'

'But you have just had a bath, and wear no make-up. You should look at yourself in a mirror.' He turned away and skilfully tipped her omelette on to a plate. Jeremy told her she was beautiful. He collected beautiful objects, antiques, paintings, ornaments—but her mother told her she was too skinny, too tall, and criticised everything she ever bought, or wore, until Jan had learned to ignore it, in sheer self defence. She smoothed back the thick tresses of honey blonde hair her mother swore was too long and thick.

'My mother *is* beautiful,' she said. 'She enjoys it when people mistake me for her younger sister.'

He laughed, then seeing her face, stopped. 'You are serious?'

'Yes.'

'Good grief! Eat your food.' He was busily making

his own omelette, breaking two eggs in a basin and beating them. Why had he been so amused at that? Jan accepted it, was used to the comments when her mother entered a room, the startled murmurs as Coral Hunter introduced Jan, always with a loving, affectionate smile towards her, as she did so. Her entrance would be ruined tonight; that was probably why she was so furious. Was it worth the rebellion?

But after next week Jan wouldn't be living with her, she would be living with Jeremy, as his wife, as Mrs Jeremy Redmayne, in a beautiful apartment overlooking Hyde Park, giving dinner parties, acting as hostess for his widowed father John Redmayne, who had an abundance of charm, and more money than he knew what to do with, and who was, in a way, very similar to her mother. Too similar. They didn't like each other very much.

She sighed. Jeremy wasn't like his father, fortunately. He had the charm, all right, but not that quality of ruthlessness. And she loved him; she really loved him. If only he understood her reluctance to go away to the Bahamas, if only he'd said all right, of course we'll go to the cottage—if—if—she probably wouldn't be here now. Those two last-minute invitations had been neither here nor there. But on top of the hurt the night before——

'Please eat.'

'I'm sorry.' She cut into the omelette obediently. 'It's delicious,' she said, after a mouthful. 'Did you put herbs in?'

'A few only, just for piquancy.' He looked at her across the table. 'You are miles away. What are you thinking? Of the phone call?'

'No. Of my fiancé.'

'As you should be. Why then do you look so unhappy?'

'I'm not. I love him.'

'You keep telling me that as if you need to reassure yourself.'

'How dare you say that!'

He shrugged. 'It is true. You do.'

'I told you before because you were *rude* enough to ask.' She laid her knife and fork down. 'I hope we're not going to have an argument again, I've had enough battles these past twenty-four hours——'

'Better now than after the wedding, when it is too late.'

'You speak as though it's a life sentence!'

'Perhaps it is. Is it not better to see things clearly now you have the chance, and are many miles away, than leave it until you have the ring on your finger? If you are making a mistake——'

'But I'm not! It was all a misunderstanding, about the honeymoon——' She broke off. She had done it again. 'I don't know why I'm talking to you like this. It's of no possible interest to you——'

'People interest me. Therefore you, and your fiancé, and your mother, interest me——'

'You're not a psychologist as well as a bricklayer, are you?' she asked with irony.

He smiled. 'Not exactly. But then I'm not exactly a bricklayer either. Is it necessary always to classify people by what they do? We are all individuals. You are an individual, you decided to come away to visit your aunt at an inconvenient time—yet it was your decision. It will possibly upset one or two people, it has certainly upset your mother, and I don't think your fiancé will be too pleased, especially not when he knows I am here, but here you are anyway, and have decided to stay. And when you return to London you will be clearer in your mind. It is obvious to me that you are very confused at the moment.'

'Good gracious!' Jan had listened to his words, to the force of them, and she wanted to laugh, to let him know how ridiculous she found them. The only thing that stopped her was the devastating truth of them. It was as though he could rip away the civilised veneer everyone wore and see what lay behind. And that made him even more frightening—in a different way.

'I surprise you? Because I say the truth?'

'Possibly.'

'What was the misunderstanding about the honeymoon?'

So she told him, and oddly enough, in the telling, it seemed even to her that she had made a mountain out of a molehill. There was a pause when she had finished. Then he spoke. 'And that was it? The reason you ran away?'

'Yes.' It was a whisper.

'Why did you not speak your mind when it was

originally decided instead of leaving it to this late stage?'

'Because—oh!' she stared at him wide-eyed. 'You wouldn't understand. It was all so gradual—my mother, Jeremy—it just seemed to have *happened*, that's all. You've not met them, you're not likely to— so how can you know?'

He shrugged. 'True. But do you always let other people run your life for you?'

'I don't! How can you——' She glared at him helplessly. 'I wouldn't have come here if I did, would I?'

'You came here hoping your aunt would soothe away the bumps for you, didn't you?'

It was too near the mark for her liking. And in that moment something changed, and she saw clearly for the first time. Saw what she should have seen months— ages—before. 'You're right,' she admitted. 'Oh, you're so right.'

'That makes a change,' he observed dryly.

'I'll phone Jeremy now, and tell him.'

'Tell him what?'

Jan paused on her way to the door. 'Why, that I was stupid to get in a panic at this late stage, when I should have spoken up before—that I'll stay here a couple of days and then go home.' She smiled. 'And I'll also tell him I'm going to be the perfect wife, but that I'll have a mind of my own!'

'He'll appreciate that,' Sandor Gregas remarked. Jan frowned, sensing sarcasm, then laughed.

'I don't care whether he does or not. He'll have to

learn to appreciate it——' and she went out.

It was Jeremy's father who answered, and he was in a worse temper than her mother had been, although Jan wouldn't have thought it possible. She listened with growing dismay to his diatribe, then slammed the telephone down, stood looking at it, and as Sandor walked out of the kitchen, turned to him and said:

'He's on his way.'

'Who. The fiancé?'

'Yes. He should be here any time——'

'Why? Is he flying?' amused, not believing.

'Oh yes, I'm afraid so. Jeremy's borrowed Daddy's helicopter—and Daddy wasn't very pleased either.' And then, as Sandor started to laugh she whirled on him.

'It's not *funny*!' she exclaimed.

'I think so. Your Jeremy flying here to rescue you from the foreign beast—he must love you.'

'You're laughing at me. Stop laughing at me!'

'Instead of losing your temper with me, had you better not prepare for his arrival? Be calm, cool, self-possessed—are you intending to return to London with him?'

'No—I don't know—I——'

'Be clear in your mind. Then stick to your decision.'

'How easy you make it sound,' she said ruefully.

'It's a start—if you really intended what you said before.'

'I did. I think—I think I shall tell him—I'm staying. At least until Monday.'

'With me.'

'At this cottage—yes.'

'And you think he will appreciate the subtle difference?'

'He trusts me,' Jan said coldly.

'Perhaps. Does he trust me?'

'How can he? He doesn't know you. Neither do I, for that matter.'

'Precisely. How do you know——'

'My aunt didn't seem concerned when I told her.'

He smiled softly. 'Your aunt is one of those rare people who sees only good. Is she the best judge of my character?'

'I don't know. Can I trust you?' She faced him, clear-eyed, saw the depths that were in him, and experienced the strangest sensation of floating.

'Yes,' he said quietly, and he wasn't smiling now.

'Then that's good enough for me.' She looked away because she sensed the strength and the force in him. She had never met a man like Sandor Gregas in her life. In all her cushioned existence, moneyed, meeting all the right people in the right places, she had never encountered anyone with such a forceful personality. 'I think I'll go and put some make-up on.'

'And I shall take the dogs out for a walk——' He lifted his hand. 'No, wait. Do you hear?'

She did, and her heart bumped. There was an unmistakable drone outside, coming nearer and nearer. She ran to the front door and looked out. The familiar red and blue helicopter hovered outside seeking a place to land. She looked at Sandor Gregas.

'You wish me to keep out of the way while you talk?'

'Yes, please.'

'I shall be in my room.' He nodded. 'Good luck.'

'Thanks.' Jan waited, hearing him run upstairs, a door closing, and turned away. The helicopter had vanished, the sound stopped. Any moment now, Jeremy was going to walk up the path, and she wondered what he would say.

'It's the most ridiculous thing I've ever heard, Jan. Ye gods! Dad's having kittens—your mother's aged ten years, and you calmly sit there drinking coffee and telling me you need a breathing space! Be reasonable, darling, we're all a bit fraught at the moment.' Jeremy ran his fingers through his hair in exasperation. Jan watched him, and it was like watching a stranger. This was the man she loved, her husband-to-be, and she felt only a huge irritation with him. It alarmed her, and to cover up, she exerted herself to be extra charming—which, judging by his words, didn't seem to be working.

She made another effort. 'Jeremy darling, I know it's hard for you to understand, but my mother is very wearing, you know——'

'It's *me* you're marrying, my sweet, or had you forgotten? She's only doing her best——'

'And you both get on like a house on fire, yes, I know that. You don't have to live with her, though. You might see a different side of her.'

'You're being disloyal!'

'If I am, I'm sorry, but it's the truth. And I'm sorry we had the row about our honeymoon. I shouldn't have made such a fuss. It's not that important.'

'What do you mean, not important? Is that how you look upon it?'

'I didn't mean *that*.' He was being difficult, and she was holding on to her temper with difficulty. 'I only meant that of course the Bahamas will be fine—I just thought it would be so lovely to be alone——'

'There'll be time for that when we come back to London,' said Jeremy firmly.

'Will there? What about your father?'

'What about him? He won't be living with us.'

'He has the apartment above—and you're very close with him.'

'Are you annoyed about that as well?'

She stood up 'Oh, good grief, Jeremy, I don't mean anything of the sort! What are you trying to do, pick a quarrel?'

'You're not doing so badly on that score,' he retorted. 'I've never known you so edgy. And your mother says there's some fellow living here as well, a damned foreigner——'

'He's a guest of Aunt Jessie's.'

'Yes. Only *she's* not here.'

'I didn't know that, or I wouldn't have come!'

'It doesn't matter anyway. You don't think I'd let you stay here alone with him, do you?' He stood up as well, resting his hands on the table, and faced her, his stance aggressive. 'Where is he anyway?'

'Upstairs, I think.'

'Then why don't *you* go upstairs, get your case, and tell him you're leaving?'

Their eyes met in a silent clash. Jan spoke with difficulty. 'Because I'm not going to that damned reception at the American Embassy tonight. And I'm tired. I'm going to have an early night—don't worry, there's a bolt on my bedroom door——'

'Good God, are you mad! Can't you see what the papers would make of this if they found out? "Heir's bride runs off to love-nest the week before the wedding." Oh *yes*, they'd love *that*. Don't be bloody stupid, Jan——'

'You're just like my mother!' she snapped. 'All *she* can think about is the damned headlines! You should be marrying her——' She stopped, aghast, and he, white-faced, looked as though she had struck him.

'That was unforgivable,' he whispered. 'Totally unforgivable!'

'I'm sorry.'

'Sorry's not enough. I find that remark very offensive. I think you'd better get your case before we both say things we'll regret.'

'I'm not going back with you,' she said.

'I don't accept that.'

'You don't have much choice.' She was trembling, all coloured drained from her face. 'Unless you intend to use force.'

'Don't make me.' Jeremy's eyes glittered. She had

never seen him so angry in all the time she had known him. His darkly tanned face was flushed, and his mouth set in a grim line. 'You're going to marry me next week —and until the wedding you're living at your own home, and that's that.' He turned. 'I'll get your case. Where is it?'

'I'm fed up with having my life taken over by you, by my mother, by your father——'

'What the hell do you mean?' He whirled round on her. 'Taken over? What the hell do you mean?' They stood a foot or so apart, and the air bristled with unbearable tension.

'You know!' she shouted. 'You already know! *I'm* not expected to make a fuss when *you* go swanning off to Cannes as you did last month——'

'That was business!' He was white round the mouth, a danger sign.

'Oh *yes*, I know. And that's why you couldn't take me, wasn't it? And I suppose I'm expected to sit at home twiddling my thumbs after we're married while you go gadding off to America and all sorts of places——'

'You knew that when we became engaged!'

'I didn't know that you'd be taking other women out to dine!' she snapped.

'What are you talking about?'

'I didn't tell you. A friend of mine, Charlotte, was in Cannes that week, and she saw you in a party dining at the Carlton—you were with that pop singer, Chantal de——'

'That was business!' he snapped.

'You already said that!' she reminded him. 'I said nothing because I trust you. It's a pity *you* don't trust *me*!'

'I do.'

'Not enough to allow me to stay here, apparently.'

'Alone—yes. With some bloody foreigner, no.'

'Oh, you mean it would be okay if he were English?' she jeered.

'No, I damn well don't mean that, and you know it.'

'Then what *do* you mean? Do you think he's going to rape me or something? You don't want your virgin bride despoiled——'

'You're talking rubbish!' She thought for a moment that Jeremy was going to strike her. He was shaking with anger, and she suddenly saw him clearly, saw the petulant lines around his mouth, the way his mouth trembled with rage—and she felt ill.

'I won't be, I promise you. I'll be all yours, Jeremy—but I'm not going back in that damned helicopter.'

He grabbed her arm and whirled her round. 'You damn well *are*!' he shouted.

'Ouch, you're hurting me!' Jan freed herself and caught him a stinging slap on his face.

'You bitch!'

'You'd better go, Jeremy,' she panted.

And a voice from the hallway said: 'Forgive my interruption, but may I make myself a cup of coffee?'

Jeremy turned, very slowly, then he looked at Jan. 'Is that him?' he demanded. She knew that voice all right. It was the voice of the public schoolboy dismissing someone so totally inferior as to be almost beyond notice. Jan shivered, suddenly cold, not with anger, but with the fear of what he might say next. He had once annihilated a careless waiter at a restaurant and left him completely shattered—in front of several dozen people. Jan had hated that, and had felt sick with humiliation. She had managed to forget it, until now. Now it came back so strongly that she felt the sickness again. Five minutes after that previous incident Jeremy had dismissed it from his mind.

She swallowed. 'This is Sandor Gregas, Jeremy,' she said. Jeremy turned his back on the waiting man and said:

'Well, my dear, go and get your case. That settles it. I'm not having you staying here with him.' He spoke as though Sandor were a piece of furniture standing in an inconvenient place in the hall.

'Do *you* want to get your case, Miss Hunter?' Sandor asked, and she could have sworn that his voice held laughter. Didn't he know? Couldn't he sense the demolition job that Jeremy was about to do?

'No, I don't,' she said. 'Do come in, Mr Gregas. Excuse my fiancé, he's rather upset.'

'Don't apologise for me, darling,' Jeremy murmured. 'I have a tongue in my head—remember?'

Sandor Gregas was behind him. 'Excuse me,' he said, with a grave courtesy. 'May I pass?' They were only inches away from each other. And suddenly Jan felt as if she couldn't breathe.

CHAPTER THREE

'Oh, certainly you may,' said Jeremy smoothly, and moved aside. He was icily polite now. 'You are staying here, Mr—er—Griggers?'

'Gregas,' said Sandor, speaking the word slowly and clearly, as if to a child. 'G-R-E-G-A-S. And your name?'

'Redmayne.'

Sandor walked over to the sink and filled the kettle. He glanced briefly at the two cups on the table. 'Do you want more coffee?'

'No, thanks.' It was Jeremy who answered, cool, oh, so very cool. 'Tell me, Mr Gregas, would you consider moving out for a few days?'

Jan's heart was bumping. She wanted to sit down, but she stayed very still, where she was. What on earth was coming now?

He paused in the act of switching on the gas. 'For what reason?'

'Because my fiancée is insisting on remaining here, for reasons best known to herself, and as her aunt is not here——' Jeremy paused.

Sandor smiled politely, a delicate questioning smile. 'Yes?' he asked.

'Surely I don't have to draw you a picture?' Jeremy's mouth lifted contemptuously. He managed to imply that he considered he was dealing with an idiot. 'It's hardly proper for you two to be alone here.'

'Perhaps not. I have, however, nowhere to go.'

'I'm sure we could find you an hotel.'

'I'm sure you could, but that would not suit me.'

'What would? Do I have to spell it out for you? Jan is Miss Ingles' niece. You—forgive my bluntness—are an absolute stranger of whom, quite frankly, we've never heard——'

'You talk about drawing pictures and spelling things out, Mr Redmayne. I find that most interesting. And the fact that you have never heard of me is hardly anything I intend to concern myself with. I have never heard of you either—but I can live with that fact.' Sandor turned his back on Jeremy and began to spoon ground coffee into the percolator.

Jan risked a look at her fiancé. Any minute now. . . .

'Are you trying to be deliberately offensive?' A nerve twitched in Jeremy's cheek.

Sandor concentrated on putting the lid on the percolator before answering. Then, satisfied, he turned to face the icily furious man. 'Offensive?' he said. 'Trying?' He seemed amused. He seemed to be having difficulty in keeping a smile off his face. 'If I *tried*, you would be in no doubt about it, I assure you. I don't consider it worth trying with someone like you. I am here, I am staying here. The only person who can ask me to leave is Miss Ingles, the owner of this house. So on that matter the subject is closed. Now, I shall take my coffee into the lounge, because I have work to do, and leave you to continue your discussion here. Perhaps, when you are ready to leave, you will let me know so that I can make sure the dogs are in. Excuse me.'

He poured out his coffee and walked towards the kitchen door, only Jeremy was blocking his exit. 'You don't walk out like that,' he snapped. 'Perhaps I haven't made myself clear. I'm telling you—not asking you—to leave this house.'

'And I have just refused. So what are you going to do about it? Use force on me as you did on your fiancée? That would not be advisable. I am not a woman, and your physical condition leaves a lot to be desired.' Sandor looked Jeremy up and down, slowly, then smiled. 'Will you let me pass?'

Jan saw what was about to happen a split second before Jeremy moved, and she shouted something, but too late. The cup of coffee went flying as Jeremy knocked it from Sandor's hand, and followed it by a punch to his jaw. It didn't connect. Even as the cup clattered to the floor and shattered, Sandor evaded the blow, weaving slightly to one side, and began to laugh.

'Don't try and fight, little man,' he said, and stepped back. 'And don't try to hit me again.'

Jeremy came forward, and Jan then knew why Sandor had moved back. As he reached the table, the Hungarian moved again, sideways, caught Jeremy's upraised arm and held it. Then, very slowly, he tightened his grip, bending the arm slowly, inexorably, until Jeremy, white-faced, was almost kneeling.

'Now,' he said, 'you will pick up the pieces of the cup you broke.' The smile had gone. Jan saw what was on his face, and she couldn't have moved if she had tried.

Jeremy made a supreme effort to break free, which only resulted in him being forced down even further, and he cried out in pain. At that, Jan darted forward and caught Sandor's other arm and pulled it.

'Stop it,' she cried. 'Oh please—stop!' She was sobbing. He released Jeremy at once, looked at her, and his eyes were like steel. She bent and began to scoop up the broken pieces from the floor, and Jeremy, white-faced and shaken, staggered to his feet, rubbing his shoulder.

He spoke in a low voice to the man, vile, unprintable words, and Sandor hit him, flat-handed, on the jaw, and said: 'Get out.'

'Don't worry, I'm going.' Jeremy had suffered more than the blow. His supreme confidence was badly bruised as well. He looked at Jan, and almost spat the words out. 'Are you coming or not? This is the last time I'll ask.'

She moved forward helplessly, drawn by the threads of anger that stretched from him, and Sandor said, very quietly, but his voice stopped her in her tracks, 'Remember, it is your life. If you go, you will be as confused as when you ran away.'

She hesitated, torn, indecisive, seeing her life stretching both ways. London—here. Turmoil—peace. Jeremy said, in a voice she had never heard, the voice of a stranger:

'If you *don't* come now, that's it. We're through!'

It was so simple. She had only to walk through the door. He loved her, or he would not have come all the way in his father's helicopter for her. He loved her, and she loved him, and in a week's time she would be his wife and this strange interlude would be forgotten. She had no choice, really. She had to go. He had delivered the ultimatum. If she didn't, there would be no wedding, and that was unthinkable. She half turned, to look at Sandor, and saw the expression on his face. She saw, and she hesitated, because his face said it all. Particularly his eyes. They held the knowledge of her— they saw inside her, to the quaking, craven coward she really was—and she knew it as if he had spoken the words. She turned back to Jeremy and said very quietly:

'That's blackmail. Don't try and blackmail me.'

He turned and walked out without another word. Jan stood rigidly where she was until she heard the front door slam closed, and as it did, her head was filled with the rushing, roaring noise that drowned out all other light and sound, and she crumpled to the floor. It seemed that she was caught before she reached it fully.

When she opened her eyes she was on the settee in the lounge, and she was alone. Another roar filled the house, but it came from outside, and it grew fainter every second. She had no more tears to weep; the unhappiness was too deep for that. It was a pain inside her, a heavy ache that filled her, and a numbness in her limbs. She wondered if she would ever move again.

'Drink this.' Sandor's voice came from beside her, and she felt his hand beneath her head, lifting it. He held a glass of water.

'He's gone?'

'Yes.'

'He said—we're through,' she whispered.

'Do you think he meant it?'

'I don't know. You shouldn't have done that.' She struggled to sit up. She could move after all—not that it seemed to matter.

'Done what?'

'Hurt him. Hit him.'

'It gave me no pleasure. Do you think it did?' he said.

'You laughed——' she began.

'Yes, I should not have laughed. I did not want to hit him, though. I did it to silence his words.'

'You—humiliated him by making him kneel——'

'That was what he deserved, no more. It was to make him pick up——'

'But you knew you were stronger——'

'How did I know?'

'It was obvious.'

'Do you prefer weak men?' he asked.

Jan shook her head and pushed the glass away. 'Please go away. Leave me alone.'

'Very well, I will.' He walked out and closed the door. The next moment she heard him call the dogs, then the front door closed, and he passed the window, not looking in. Now she was truly alone. She had many things to think about, none pleasant. Sandor

Gregas was a strange man, a frightening, controlled man, and he could look at her and see what she was thinking, which made him—dangerous.

The cottage had three bedrooms, the third little more than a boxroom, and it was full of the accumulated clutter of Jessie Ingles' busy much-travelled life. Downstairs, as well as kitchen, lounge and dining room there was a washroom and walk-in pantry. It was a compact, warm house with beautiful antique furniture and an atmosphere of love and quiet. Gradually Jan absorbed some of this ambience and became calmer inside. With Jeremy's departure, some of her inner turmoil had subsided.

An hour had passed, and the Hungarian had not yet returned with the dogs. It was nearly teatime. She wondered what was going on in London. Jeremy would undoubtedly have contacted her mother. The telephone would shortly ring—that was inevitable. She went into the kitchen to prepare a meal, found the potatoes and some chops and started work. Before doing so, she took off her engagement ring. She looked at it before putting it down at the side of the sink. Tears filled her eyes, and some of the empty ache returned. It was a gorgeous solitaire diamond, and it had been chosen by Jeremy with love. Their engagement party had been a glorious affair at the Dorchester, a day of perfect happiness at which even her mother had gracefully taken a back seat.

And now, was it all over? Was this to be the end of

it—a sordid brawl in a kitchen, an ultimatum, Jeremy storming off, humiliated and angry? It could not be. She put the ring safely down, eyes blurred with tears, and began to peel the potatoes.

She was thus engaged when she heard the door open and the two dogs skittering down the hall, then Sandor's voice. 'Hello. You are preparing food? Good. Will there be enough for me?'

'Of course.' She turned. 'Chops and chips okay?'

'That sounds very nice.' The wind had blown his hair, and he smelt of outdoors, and looked superbly healthy. 'You are feeling better?'

'A little, thanks.'

'Do you need any help?'

'No.'

'Then I shall do some work in the lounge until it is ready.' Jan had seen some blueprints and papers on the table by the window, but she had neither looked at them nor touched them, not because she was un-interested but simply because she considered it on a par with reading others' letters, simply not done.

'Does your work concern the house you're working on?'

'Yes, indirectly. Will you excuse me?'

'Of course.' He didn't want to talk about it, and it was none of her business, but she was intrigued as to why a workman should have the plans of a house. Perhaps he was the foreman. She didn't know enough about house building anyway. She dismissed the subject from her mind, beginning to worry about the telephone call, anticipating its shrill ring at any minute, building herself to such a pitch that she began to wish it would ring, and get it over with.

She put the chops under the grill and cleared away the potato peelings, then went to find the chip pan.

Her mother's timing was perfect. Even as she set the plates on the table and went to find Sandor, the telephone rang. She shouted him, said: 'It's ready,' and picked up the telephone.

'Hello.'

'Hello, Jan dear.' Her mother was at her most dangerous when she spoke in the sweet low tones she was using now. At least it prepared her for the worst. She gripped the receiver more tightly, and listened, and listened—and listened. Nothing was said regarding Jeremy's ignominious departure—he might not have mentioned it. What emerged most clearly was his opinion of Sandor Gregas, his despair at Jan's stubborn and stupid attitude—and it was that which her mother concentrated all her force upon.

It was also quite clear to Jan that her mother, who would shortly be going to a reception at the American Embassy, was determined not to lose her temper—a thing she knew from past experience would be damaging to her looks. And even as she realised that fact, she saw things in perspective. She saw exactly where her mother's priorities lay, perhaps always had. Jan came a poor second to Coral's career. In a strange way, it helped.

She cut short a sentence of her mother's dealing with

her—Jan's—basic ingratitude, all delivered in the same sweetly reasonable voice, to ask:

'You'll be leaving soon for the Embassy do, won't you?'

'Yes. Why do you ask?' Suspicion coloured her words. She didn't like being thrown off course by an apparently irrelevant question.

'I just wondered. It does mean you won't be dashing down here tonight. Is Jeremy going as well?'

'He can hardly go without you, darling, can he?' Her mother's voice sharpened. 'What do you mean about me dashing down there?'

'Nothing. I thought Jeremy might send you to talk to me.'

'Nobody *sends me* anywhere. I had thought of coming, but there doesn't seem much point as you're so stupidly stubborn. That man had better not touch you, that's all—you realise he'll know *who* you are, don't you?'

'He should do. I told him who you were.'

'He was abominably rude to me on the telephone before. You're quite mad! Jeremy was most upset—in fact if I were you I'd start driving back now. You can phone him when you reach London.'

'But you're not me, are you?'

'I'm not sure what you mean, Jan,' snapped her mother, 'but I don't like your tone. Some madness has come over you, and I don't like it.'

'Mother, you'll be late if you keep talking. I'll phone you tomorrow and let you know I'm still all right——'

There was a small silence, during which Jan could almost see her mother glancing at the clock, torn between her duty and what she really wanted to do. Then:

'You don't have any—er—doubts, do you?'

'Heavens no, he's assured me he's not going to rape me——' A muffled shriek nearly tore the line.

'Jan! For God's sake, girl—oh, my God!' her mother wailed.

'Don't distress yourself. I was only reassuring you,' said Jan.

'Which means you've been talking—oh, he was right, Jeremy was right—what are we going to do?'

'Why, what about?' Jan was nearly enjoying the conversation. She hadn't expected such a shocked reaction.

'The man—he said he looked a beast. That's it! That does it. You can't stay——'

'Don't be stupid, Mother,' said Jan, and put the telephone down.

She went into the kitchen, picked up a chip and ate it. She looked at Sandor. 'I've upset my mother,' she said. 'She'll call back any moment.'

'Yes. Shall we put your food to keep warm?'

'I think so——' The telephone interrupted her. 'Ah, there she is.'

'Hello.'

'Now you are not to hang up on me, do you hear? I'm trying to keep very calm, but you're making it difficult. You're to listen to me—are you there?'

'I'm listening, Mother.'

'I've decided, and it's *quite impossible* for you to stay there at all, any longer. It's now nearly six. If you set off in half an hour, you'll be home by ten or so. I'll leave some supper for you, and I'll phone Jeremy and tell him——'

'No.'

'I will not accept no! I'm *telling* you, my girl, you're coming home tonight.'

'And if I don't?'

'Then I shall no longer consider you as my daughter. I hope I make myself very clear, Jan. This will no longer be your home—I shall not attend the wedding——'

'Didn't Jeremy tell you? If I don't come home, there isn't going to be a wedding to attend.'

The shocked silence told her her answer. Jan went on quickly before she could think about whether she would regret her words: 'So you see, that's two of you blackmailing me. Would *you* let anybody blackmail *you*?'

'It is not blackmail. It's a statement of fact.' Her anger vibrated down the line. 'Think well before you answer. You'll have no money, no home—nothing. I've decided, and I never go back on my word.'

'I know you don't, Mother.' Jan's whole world was crumbling around her. So why should there be this faint but unescapable feeling of relief? 'I'm sorry, very sorry.' She blinked away the tears.

'As you should be. I've been waiting for you to

come to your senses and apologise——'

'You don't understand. I'm not apologising. I'm sorry that you made this decision, because I'm staying here.'

The line went dead, the dialling tone began and, shaken, Jan replaced the receiver. She felt like a person drowning, seeing her whole life flash past before her. It was the worst moment of her life. It was worse than anything she had ever known before. She didn't want to face Sandor, or to eat. She wanted oblivion, a merciful escape. There was no escape from this situation, none at all. She had to go on living, she had to, somehow, get through the next twenty-four hours, and then the next, and the next. . . .

She walked slowly up the stairs and into her bedroom, sat down by the window and gazed out, seeing nothing of the sea crashing against the rocks, her whole body numbed with the shock of what had happened.

Minutes passed; they might have been hours. She heard footsteps, then a tap on the door, but it seemed to have nothing to do with her, and she didn't answer.

She saw a vague shape in the dressing table mirror, but it was too much effort to move. Then she felt two hands on her shoulders and looked up at the mirror to see Sandor's reflection.

'It is bad?' he said.

Jan closed her eyes, and didn't speak. He pulled her gently to her feet and turned her round to face him. Still numbed, she stood there limp, unresisting, and he put his arms around her and held her to him. There was nothing sexual in it. It was the gesture of a parent comforting a child, and she sensed the leashed strength within him, the controlled gentleness, and was warmed by it.

'My mother has finished with me,' she said, in a toneless voice.

She felt him move, heard his indrawn breath, then he said quietly, his voice soft against her ear: 'Give me your mother's number. I will telephone her, I will tell her I am leaving, and then I will go from here tonight.'

The warmth of his body filled her with a strength she badly needed. She clung to him, unaware of what she was doing until she realised her arms were round him and her face was against his chest. And there was nothing wrong in it, no guilt, because for that moment he was her anchor and her strength.

'It wouldn't do any good.' Her voice was muffled, but she knew he heard. 'Once she decides, that's it.'

'It is not too late. Tell me exactly what she said.' He led her to the bed and sat her down, then sat beside her. It seemed the most natural thing in the world for him to put his right arm around her waist and hold her. 'Tell me,' he repeated.

Slowly, almost word for word, Jan told him, and when she had finished he said: 'Then I shall do it. The problem—that is, me—will have vanished. You see?'

She turned her face towards him, the bright tears filling her eyes and spilling down her cheeks. Sandor touched them with his finger and gently brushed them away. 'Do not cry any more,' he said. 'I am helping you.'

'I know.' She felt safe, safer than she ever had before in her life. Why it should be so she did not question; it was, quite simply, a fact. Here, with him, a perfect stranger, she felt more secure than she ever had with her mother, or with Jeremy. 'Thank you.' She did something instinctively and naturally—she put her hand to his cheek and stroked it. Sandor closed his eyes, then he caught hold of her hand, put it to his mouth and kissed her palm. And still there was nothing save warmth, and the reassurance she so desperately needed.

She made a little murmur, and he released her hand, very slowly. Jan looked at it, looked where he had kissed, and smiled. 'That was nice,' she said. She blinked the tears away. 'I feel better already.'

'Do you? Had I not better ring now?'

'Yes. I'll come down with you and dial the number.'

'And you will eat your tea while I do so?'

'I'll try.' She looked at him. 'Where will you go?'

He shrugged. 'Anywhere. I can sleep at the new house—there is a room completed downstairs. I can take some bedding——'

'Oh no!' She was horrified.

'Why?' He looked surprised. 'That is nothing, I assure you.'

'But—I—I can't let you do that,' she stammered.

'I cannot go to an hotel. I must work here every day.'

'Oh, of course. I'm sorry, I'd forgotten that. It seems

so awful——' She was anguished.

'It is the solution. Before—I will be honest—when your fiancé ordered me to go, I refused, because I do not like orders. But now this is different. I cannot under any circumstances be the cause of such a dreadful thing between you and your mother—you understand?'

'Yes, I understand. Thank you.' He stood up and helped her to her feet, steadying her, taking her arm. She stumbled over the rug, and it was as well he held her or she would have fallen. She landed against him, breathless—looked up, saw that which was in his eyes, and the smile died away. His eyes held hers and she felt herself drawn towards him, drowning in what she had glimpsed for that moment before he could hide it. . . .

Their lips touched, and it was as inevitable as the night following day—it was as inevitable as everything else that had been before. They melted together in a warmth that filled the world; his mouth searched hers, and the hunger was abated, the strength and fire of him filled her, and his arms were around her, so strong, yet gentler than anything she had known. And the next, too, was inevitable, the movement towards the bed, the sinking down on it so that they lay against each other, touching all the way, afire with such warmth as she had never known. Sandor's hands were gentle and light, butterfly light, his face against hers cool and hard, his lips a gentle fire.

There was no time, there was nothing save what she was experiencing, a joy and ecstasy complete in a kiss.

He murmured something, she didn't hear it, she moved, whispered: 'What?' and he repeated it.

'This is madness. We must stop now——'

'I know——' Then all sound was lost as he kissed her again, a long, lingering deep kiss of sensual searching. Beautiful, perfect.

It was the last one. He pulled himself away, and he was trembling. 'No more,' he said thickly. He sat on the edge of the bed and rubbed his face.

Jan came back to sanity more swiftly. The awful thing was that she felt not a trace of guilt. She sat up and buttoned her blouse, then rose and went over to the dressing table, where she brushed her hair vigorously, turned to the man who sat like a statue on the bed, and said: 'I think—we'd better forget——' she faltered—'what just happened.'

He looked up then, turned slowly, looked at her. 'Forget?' he repeated quietly. 'Ah yes, how simple. Come, to the telephone before I forget what I promised myself——' and he walked out, leaving her standing, hairbrush in hand, confused, still disorientated.

She put the brush away and followed him down to the hall. He moved aside for her to pick up the telephone, which she did, and dialled her mother's number. Silently she handed it to him as it began to ring. Then she waited, tense, with dry mouth, as it rang, and rang, and rang. . . .

Sandor looked. 'No reply.'

'There must be.' She bit her lip. 'Keep trying——' She was stopped as he held up a warning hand, and spoke.

'Hello? Mrs Hunter? Oh, I see. Do you know when she will be back?' It would be the housekeeper. Jan motioned to him, and he handed her the receiver.

'Mrs Jessup? It's me—Jan. Has my mother gone to the reception?'

The housekeeper sounded distressed. 'Oh, Jan, I don't know what to say.' She was nearly weeping, that much was obvious. 'She's gone off in a very bad way— I know it's none of my business, but it's been a terrible day since you left this morning——' Jan listened. She got on well with the quiet, efficient Mrs Jessup, who was well enough paid by her mother to keep her job in spite of the difficulties of working for a perfectionist. Jan knew it involved the older woman occasionally biting her tongue, for she had an elderly mother she supported, and needed the money. She felt wretched that Mrs Jessup's distress was almost certainly her fault.

'And when she went, she was saying awful things about you——'

'I know. Please don't be upset. What time did she say she'd be back?'

'About midnight. She said I could go to bed, and not wait up—she said—if you phoned, I was to hang up.'

'Oh God,' said Jan. 'Look, don't say I phoned. I'll try at twelve. Just don't say anything.'

'I don't think it'll do much good. She was very determined.'

That seemed to be an understatement. Jan sighed. 'I know. But I'll try anyway. Thanks, Mrs Jessup. Goodbye.' She replaced the receiver.

'I'll have to try later,' she said. 'She'll be back at midnight.' She looked at Sandor. 'Six hours to go.'

'Yes. What do you intend to do?'

'I don't know. Go out for a drive somewhere. I can't sit around waiting.' She shrugged helplessly. 'It's all so awful. And it's all my fault.'

He shook her roughly, suddenly angry. 'Don't say that. You blame yourself, but you are wrong to do that. You hear me?—wrong!'

She was shocked by his vehemence, but it shook her out of her mood.

'Right, it's not my fault.' Her eyes glittered. 'The heck with them all! I'm going out—would you like to come?' She might as well compound her felony.

'That would be very nice,' he said, smiling. 'Yes, I would.'

CHAPTER FOUR

I MIGHT as well be hanged for a sheep as for a lamb, Jan thought. She changed from blouse and jeans into long skirt and lacy top, slipped on her sandals, applied lipstick with a steady hand, and looked at herself in the mirror. 'The bride-to-be,' she murmured, 'going out with another man.' A reckless sense of excitement filled her, heady, stimulating. One week ago, even a day or so ago, she would never have visualised a bizarre situation like this. She had always been totally faithful to Jeremy, ever since the day, one year ago, that she had become engaged to him. She wondered if he had been equally loyal. She had often wondered that—— Her speculation was cut short by a knock at her door.

'I'm ready,' she said, and picked up her handbag. She opened the bedroom door, and for a second—just a split second—she didn't recognise the man who stood before her. Gone were the jeans, the checked shirt with rolled-up sleeves. He looked vastly different, in cream rollnecked sweater and black pants. He carried a black jacket, one finger hooked, jacket over shoulder.

'Let's go,' he said. 'One problem. Unless you like travelling in a lorry we will have to go in your car.'

'But I was anyway.' She had to smile at the thought of clambering up into an enormous lorry. 'Why? You're not one of those men who doesn't like a woman driver, are you?'

'No.' He seemed surprised.

'Well then.' It was better, so much better not to remember; to pretend that nothing had happened. It had
been a moment of madness, following despair. And it
would never happen again. 'Let's go, shall we?'

They locked the doors and windows, leaving the well
fed dogs resting in the lounge, and went out into a
warm summer evening. Jan turned and drove slowly
down the track. As they passed the unfinished building,
she said: 'It's going to be a beautiful house. Do you
know the people who're going to live there?'

'Yes.' He smiled. 'Or rather, should I say the person.
It is me.'

She nearly skidded up the bank, righted the car.
'Oh!' She laughed. She had never thought she would
laugh again. 'It's yours. You're building your own
house?'

'With some expert help, yes. You find that strange?'

'No, I just didn't expect——' She stopped. How did
you say, without being offensive, that he had looked
like a workman? He certainly didn't now.

'You must think I'm stupid,' she apologised. 'But
why didn't you say before?'

'It didn't seem necessary. You have enough to think
about.'

'So you must have bought the land from my aunt?'

'Yes. And she invited me to stay, and work from her
house. As I had no home I accepted with pleasure. She
is a very charming woman.'

'She is. I love her very much.' They were near the

main road now, and four miles along was a pub. 'Shall we have a drink? There's a pub along the road.'

'I know. I take Aunt Jessie there sometimes in the evenings.'

'In your lorry?' she asked mischievously.

'No.' He laughed. 'My car is in a garage being serviced at the moment. I shall have it back on Monday.'

She wondered what kind of a car he would have. A nifty Jaguar sports? Likely. 'What do you run?' she asked.

'A Lamborghini.'

What else? she thought. The man was full of surprises. But there were more to come. 'Very nice.' She glanced briefly at him.

'But not practical in London traffic.'

'No, I know what you mean.' She sighed, then realised. 'You come from London?'

'Not originally, but I have lived there for four years. Soon I shall be living here.'

They neared the pub, and Jan drove into the car park, which was practically empty. It was a true village type pub, no concession made to passing trade, which meant a satisfying lack of horse brasses and twee lamps. They went in to see a few locals from the village down the road, and a cheerful barman greeted Sandor like an old friend.

Jan sat in a corner, and suddenly experienced a rush of sadness as she remembered. When he brought the drinks over she looked at him, and he saw, and he knew.

'Smile,' he said. 'Even if you don't feel like smiling.'

'I'll try.' She tried. It didn't take the pain away, but you couldn't cry if you were smiling. 'Cheers.' She didn't want to think about her own problems. 'Your job—will you work here—at the house, I mean?'

'I can do. I am an architect. I prefer country to city. I will travel up once a week to my office to see that everything goes well, and the rest of the time I shall work at my new home.'

'Won't your boss mind?'

'I have no boss.'

'You—you mean—*you're* the boss?'

'Yes.' He smiled.

'Good grief! You must think me an awful fool—I thought——'

'I know what you thought, but it did not matter to me. I know also what your fiancé thought. No, forgive me, I wasn't going to mention him.'

'It doesn't matter.' Jan shook her head. 'He's very public school, you know. I don't think anyone has ever spoken to him like you did.'

'I told a lie when I said I had never heard of him. In a way I had. My firm has done work for his father.' He looked at her. 'You know the saying, it's a small world —that applies. I know his father very well.'

'Good grief,' she said faintly. 'Any more surprises?'

'Perhaps—a few. Drink your gin and I'll get you another.'

'I didn't come out for you to buy me drinks, you know,' she protested.

'I know. We came out for a ride. But another drink won't hurt, then I shall drive you somewhere nice.'

'You'll drive *me*?' she murmured.

'Yes. It won't matter if I get stopped. Two lagers is hardly anything—but two gins——' he shook his head as if shocked, and she found herself laughing.

'I've only had one!'

'I insist you have another. For medicinal reasons.'

Suddenly it seemed pointless to argue. Jan felt as if she were being taken care of, in the nicest way, and it was new, and she liked it, and decided to go along with it. 'All right. Thank you.'

Sandor went over to the bar, to return with two more glasses which he set down on the table. She looked up at him, and wondered what would have happened if she had met him eighteen months ago, instead of Jeremy. Her heart was doing little erratic bumps, and she remembered his touch, his caresses—his kisses— and she was warm, and frightened of her own reaction. Jeremy had sensed the danger she had not then imagined. Perhaps, after all, he was right. Perhaps she should have gone back to London. . . .

'And what are you worrying about now?' he asked, and she felt the warmth creep into her face.

'I should have gone back, shouldn't I?' she said. She looked into those eyes that saw everything, saw the flicker of awareness in them; he knew.

'That will not happen again.' His voice was deeper, almost harsh. 'Now that I know——' he stopped.

She felt stifled. 'Know what?'

'About myself. I was—have always prided myself
on my self-control.' He seemed to be having difficulty
in finding the right words. 'I was mistaken. Now—all
the more reason I should go——'

'Yes.' She trembled, because she knew as well. 'I
don't make a habit of kissing strange men, or even
allowing myself to be kissed—although I'm not sure if
you'll believe it, but it does happen to be the truth.'

'I believe you,' he answered. 'I meant only to comfort you in your distress. But I think you know that.'
Jan couldn't deny it to herself any longer. She found
him physically magnetic. She was drawn to him ir-
resistibly and hopelessly. If he took her in the car now
and started to kiss her again she knew she would not
only not resist, but respond in a way she never had
with Jeremy or any of her previous men friends. She
was shocked and horrified at herself, yet she knew it
was so. He had touched her, and made her realise what
it was like to be a woman. And he was dangerous because of it. And she was endangered. Sandor had
awoken a response in her that she didn't know existed——

'Tell me about yourself,' she said. 'When did you decide that you'd had enough of London?'

'A year ago. Once I had made up my mind, I set out
looking for a place—and found this one.' He smiled.
'That was it. I talked to your aunt, found the land belonged to her, that she was willing to sell to me, and we
went from there.'

'She never told me. She never said a word. Yet I've

seen her several times in the past twelve months——'

'I know why,' he interrupted. 'I asked her not to tell anyone——' he hesitated. 'I had—several reasons.'

Jan desperately wanted to know. 'Please—I don't want to pry,' she said, but she ached, because suddenly she sensed that there was a woman involved, and she was shocked at her own surge of emotion.

He shrugged. 'They are boring reasons. Shall we go?' It was as if a shutter had come down. It was softened with a smile.

'Of course.' She finished her second drink, and stood up. She opened her bag. 'Here are the keys. I'm just going to the Ladies. I'll see you outside.' She walked away without a backward glance.

She stared at her face in the mirror of the small Ladies' room. Her eyes were large and dark. She felt as if she were on the brink of something unknown. She touched her face. It was not too late. She should drive back to London, ask her mother's forgiveness—she should phone Jeremy and do the same. She took a deep breath. And then it would all be the same as before. Only it wouldn't. Because one man had stepped into her life, and because of him she could see things clearly, perhaps for the first time. She saw the emptiness of her wealthy, cushioned existence, she caught a glimpse of another world. A world in which you made your own decisions and stuck to them, and went ahead. . . .

She picked up her bag and walked out, into the car park. Sandor had driven her Jaguar to the door, and as he saw her he leaned over to open her passenger door.

She slid in. 'Thank you. Where are we going?'

'Wait and see.' He glanced at her, then drove out on to the main road. 'Your petrol is low. We will call at a garage, I think, and get more.'

'Of course.' She opened her bag, and he said:

'I will buy it.'

'No.' She shook her head. 'That's silly. It was nice of you to buy me those drinks, but this is *my* car, even if you're driving.'

'I think you said you had come out without much money?'

'I've enough for a few gallons.'

'Then you can pay me back when you leave, if you wish. Until then, please, no more talk of money. It is something I find very boring.' But he said it as though he found the subject amusing.

Jan sighed. It was definitely different. From Jeremy —or even from her mother, she would have earned a lecture on always carrying enough, or your cheque book. . . . No, she thought, comparisons are odious, and do no good anyway. 'Then we'll change it. You de-signed your house yourself?'

'Yes. It is something I have had in mind for some time. But until I found the right place——' Sandor shrugged. 'I have now found it. The view is something quite spectacular. And the beach is ideal for sunbathing —and I enjoy swimming very much.'

'There can be some treacherous currents when the tide's going out,' she told him.

'I know. I am an extremely cautious man, Jan, I

promise you. I swim only when the tide is coming in—
and I enjoy surfing too.'

'You do?' Her eyes lit up. 'That's something I've
never tried.'

'Then you shall. The breakers are ideal. It was only
with great difficulty that I dissuaded your aunt from
having a go.'

She began to laugh. 'Honestly? I can imagine Aunt
Jessie surfing—you wouldn't need to worry, she's tried
most other things. She'd probably do as well as you.'

He joined with her laughter. 'Why do you think I
didn't let her?'

'Can I have a try?'

'Of course. Tomorrow?'

'Why not? Oh, I've no swimsuit——'

'Your aunt has several. They may be a little old-
fashioned—no bikinis, I fear—but sufficient. And if
you like water-skiing, you can do some of that too. Can
you pilot a boat?'

'Yes. Don't tell me——'

'I have one parked behind my new house. But it is
impossible to water-ski alone, you understand.'

Jan felt as if the sun had suddenly broken from behind a cloud. It was absurd, just because of a few casual
words, yet it was so. The sheer joy of living that he
exuded infected her in a way she could never have
imagined. Life was a serious business—that much she
had had instilled in her from an early age. Even leisure
pursuits were carried out with a purpose. Whether of
meeting the right people, or making profitable business

contacts, or mounting the social ladder—Jan was used to it, and had accepted it because she knew no other way. And with Jeremy there would be no alteration, for his mind revolved in a similar way to her mother's.

Yet here was a man who clearly did things because he enjoyed doing them, and who had left London because he preferred life in the country.

'You're on,' she smiled.

They were nearing a country hotel, and Sandor slowed, then said: 'I thought it would be nice to have a meal. Would you like that?'

'I would. That would be lovely, thank you.'

'No need to thank me. It is my pleasure.' He glanced at her as he slid the car skilfully into a vacant space in the crowded grounds. Then he switched off the engine. 'You are needing something to take you out of yourself, I think. Time to be serious when we return home —until then, we will have a pleasant evening.'

When we return home, he said, as though that was where they were going. As though it were the most natural thing in the world. As though they lived there together. Jan found her hands were clenched tightly in her lap. She was scarcely aware of him getting out until she felt her door opening, and he stood there.

'Are you ready?'

'Yes.' She slid out and he slammed the door shut. For a moment or two they stood there, and they were close, and she had to look up at him, and she saw the flecks of darker grey in his eyes, saw the laughter lines round them, saw the sheer strength of the man, and knew a sense of warmth and comfort she had never experienced before. He touched her arm lightly.

'Come,' he said.

Together they walked into the large reception hall, brightly lit, red-carpeted, golden wall lights and people talking, walking, or sitting and waiting. The place was cheerful, not noisy but not quiet, and from somewhere there came faint music.

'There is dancing as well,' said Sandor. 'If you wish, after we have eaten.'

Why not? she thought. I've already burnt a few boats—or bridges, or whatever it is you burn. I can only be shot once.

But she hadn't danced with him—then.

The meal was excellent in every respect, and after it they drank coffee in the ballroom, sitting in a quiet corner, watching the couples dancing to the music. Throughout the meal their conversation flitted around safe topics. Sandor had told her of his life in London, and the people he knew, and the places he had been; he was witty, and well informed, and several times she had laughed, and forgotten all about why she was there. . . .

Then, when their meal was digested, he looked at her. The band was beginning a waltz. 'Would you like to dance?' he asked.

'Yes, I'd love to.' She knew he wouldn't be as good as Jeremy. Jeremy was the expert *par excellence*, slimmer and lighter, and Sandor was a big man who was probably very much at home building or designing houses, and surfing—but it wasn't important, because she would enjoy dancing with him, just for a few minutes, that was all ... just one dance. ...

But it wasn't quite as she had expected. As he took her in his arms she felt the strange stirring in her, her body tingled, and they moved across the semi crowded floor as if they alone were there, and what Sandor lacked in expertise he made up for in sensuality, smooth, rhythmic—exciting to dance with.

The waltz finished, the band paused, and somehow, as if by mutual accord, they stood poised, waiting for the next. It was a contrast, a hot rock number, and they laughed, looked at one another, and swung into it as if they had rehearsed it for weeks.

It was exhilarating and exhausting, and at the end, Jan gasped: 'Enough! Can we sit down for a moment?' Because she knew they were going to be dancing again, and Sandor answered that of course they must sit down, and perhaps have a drink before they took to the floor again. They sat there just watching and Jan sipped her vodka Martini and felt more relaxed than she had done for ever. ...

It was nearly eleven when they finished a samba and returned to their chairs, and Sandor looked at Jan. 'We must go soon, you know, if we are to arrive home at twelve.'

She looked at him. She had lost count of time. Her head was pleasantly muzzy from a few vodkas—she wasn't sure how many. Sandor had drunk very little, just a few glasses of wine, and smoked a cigar, and he looked as cool and calm as when they had gone in. Yet Jan tingled with a kind of all-over excitement, and for a moment didn't know why they must be home at twelve. Then she remembered.

'Oh yes, of course,' she said. 'Just one more dance?'

'As you wish.' He smiled. A waltz was beginning and they got up, and it was like the first dance, only there was a difference now. He held her more closely, subtly, his lips touching her hair, and their bodies melting together as one, and a fire was there, a quickening, sensuous awareness was there, a blending. Jan wanted the waltz to go on for ever because it was too wonderful to ever finish, and she had never known anything like it before.

Then, too cruelly soon, the music stopped, Sandor shrugged almost as if in apology, and said: 'No more. Come, let us go.'

Outside she shivered in the cool night air as they walked towards the car, and when she stumbled slightly he took her arm, then her hand, and held it firmly.

There was no moon, only stars, and the lights from the hotel were left behind as they reached the car, and there it was pitch black. Jan waited for him to open the door and said: 'I've had a lovely evening. Thank you.'

The lock clicked. Sandor removed the keys, put them in his pocket, put his hands on her arms. His face was a grey shadowy blur, but his nearness was all powerful, all strength. 'So have I. Thank you for making it so,' he said, and he bent his head and kissed her very gently on the mouth. His hands were still on her arms, then, very slowly, almost reluctantly, but as if compelled, he slid them round her body until she was tightly in his embrace, and the gentle kiss turned to fire and she was burning, burning. . . .

An aching and a longing filled her and she sensed, and revelled in, the deep throb of excitement which filled him as it filled her; she slid her arms round his neck and held him as tightly as he held her. There was an eternity, there was all the world, and it was timeless, yet for ever; their bodies burned together and melted, and there was only a growing wonder and excitement of it all, and nothing else existed save the two of them.

Timeless, until—Sandor muttered something and pulled himself free, and he was trembling. 'Forgive me,' he said, his voice low and shaken, and she touched his cheek with gentle fingers and murmured huskily :

'There's nothing to forgive.'

'I want you,' he said. 'I want you very much—but you know that, don't you?'

'Yes.' A mere whisper.

'But I have promised, and I will keep my promise. You must not let me touch you again.' He opened the door for her. 'Please—get in now.'

She slid in, and he closed the door and went round to his own. Inside, he looked at her in the darkened car. 'One of us must be strong,' he said. 'Perhaps it will have to be me.' He put the keys in the ignition and Jan caught his hand before he could turn them.

'Wait,' she said.

'No, we must go. I dare not—I must not touch you

here. Please take your hand away.'

Recklessness filled her. 'No,' she said. He reached out his other hand and took hers from his.

'Yes.' She could feel still the fine tremor in his hands. 'You don't know what you're doing to me—or perhaps you do.'

'Perhaps I do.' She began to laugh—then the laughter changed to tears, and it was no longer funny. It was no longer amusing because she should not have been out enjoying herself with a strange man practically on the eve of her wedding, of her new life with Jeremy—although that seemed in doubt after the scene that afternoon. But his ultimatum had been uttered in extreme anger. Weddings weren't cancelled because of one quarrel—at least, not the kind of wedding that theirs would be, with all the press there, and a lot of the top people as guests, and good publicity all round for Redmayne Productions Ltd., and Zesty-Cola. The union of two important families—she had read it all in the magazines, in the gossip columns of the papers, and remembered most vividly the photograph of her and Jeremy taken a few weeks previously at a ball at the Grosvenor Hotel. The words beneath seemed to sum up the whole situation very neatly. She had been mildly amused, not annoyed, at the time. 'The Pop with the Fizz?' had been the eye-catching headline, then: 'Could be the union of the year when Jeremy Redmayne, heir to the vast popular record empire, ties the knot in a short while with gorgeous Jan Hunter, daughter of Mrs Zesty-Cola herself, Coral

Hunter. No, folks, that's not Zesty pop they're sipping, but vintage champagne.... what else for these two beautiful lovebirds?'

She was used to the treatment, and she knew, with a sudden pang, that in a way both her mother and Jeremy had been right. The papers would be delighted to get hold of a story like this. She was totally irresponsible, and foolish.

'Don't cry,' said Sandor. 'It disturbs me.'

'Yes, I know. It doesn't do me much good either,' she answered. 'I've been very stupid. We'd better go.'

Without another word he started up the car. They drove back to the cottage in silence, Jan absorbed in her own oppressive thoughts, Sandor concentrating on his driving. She was sick at heart. It would have been far better to have stayed watching television—or to have gone out on her own in the car. Too late now for wishful thinking—but it was better they were never too close again. Jan had no illusions. Sandor was a very physical animal. Twice he had proved it, and twice was too much. She looked at her watch. Nearly twelve. Her mouth went dry. How utterly idiotic she was! If her mother had gone to bed ... if ... it mustn't be too late, it mustn't!

'How much further?' she asked.

'Four miles, no more. We will soon be home.' Sandor didn't look at her as he spoke. He might have been angry; it was hard to tell. Jan imagined he would be a man with a hell of a temper. She had seen a small example with his treatment of Jeremy, and he hadn't even been trying then. Dear God, she thought, I should never have come—and that was a thought that had arrived too late as well.

The car began to slow, imperceptibly, and she looked at him. 'What——' she began, and he pointed to the petrol gauge. 'Oh no! We forgot!'

'*I* forgot,' he said. 'I meant to.'

'How much further?' He drew in at the side of the road and switched off.

'Two miles, that is all. We must walk.'

'Half an hour. It's nearly twelve now.'

'Yes. The sooner we go, the better. I will bring some petrol from the house tomorrow. I have a spare can in the new garage.'

'My mother——' she began.

'I know. Get out, I will lock your door.'

Jan scrambled out and slammed her door, not waiting for him, starting to walk quickly in her high-heeled sandals, almost running. Sandor caught her up, and touched her arm. 'No sense in breaking your neck,' he said.

'I want—if she's gone to bed she won't answer. She never does.'

'Then we must hope she hasn't.' His stride was longer than hers, effortless, whereas she was already breathless trying to keep up.

'Go on ahead,' she said. 'I'll give you the number.'

'And leave you walking alone? Do I look so stupid?'

'There's no one about——'

'There is no point in wasting breath discussing it

either.' He caught her hand. 'I will help you along.' He glanced at her now. 'If we are too late, I shall telephone in the morning.'

'You don't know my mother,' she said dryly.

'I feel as though I do.' His voice held a strange undertone, and she didn't want to ask what he meant, because she sensed she already knew. She had never felt as unhappy as she was at that moment for a long time.

She had a stitch in her side from trying to keep up with him, and she hated him, and at the same time felt obscurely angry with him, as though it were all his fault—which was absurd and illogical. She pulled her hand free and pressed it to her side. Sandor stopped. 'What is it?'

'I've got a stitch in my side. My legs aren't as long as yours, you know.'

'Take those shoes off and walk barefoot. The road is smooth. They weren't designed for walking. No wonder you ache!' He sounded impatient, unfriendly, and he was very probably totally fed up with the whole situation. Jan snatched them off and marched ahead. Damn you, damn you! she muttered inwardly, and wondered when the nightmare would end.

But it had only just begun.

CHAPTER FIVE

THE telephone shrilled and shrilled, and Jan could visualise it ringing out in the empty house, and behind the closed door of her mother's bedroom, her mother lying flat out, two sleeping pills inside her already taking effect, telephone bell switched off. It was twelve-twenty.

Sandor looked at her. 'No reply,' he said.

She shook her head. 'Then it will have to be in the morning,' she whispered—but he suddenly held up his hand as if to silence her.

'Hello? Ah, is Mrs Hunter there, please?' She put her ear next to Sandor's and he held it away slightly for her to hear. It was not Mrs Jessup who had answered, it was a man who was at that moment saying:

'—Who is that speaking?' Jan recognised the voice, and in a moment of inspiration snatched the receiver from Sandor and said quickly:

'Donald? It's me—Jan. Is Mother there?'

'Jan?' He sounded surprised. 'I thought there was someone else—yes, hang on a minute. She's in the kitchen. I'll go and fetch her.' The phone was put down, and Jan cupped her hand over the mouthpiece and said:

'I recognised the voice. It's a business friend of my mother's. I'm sorry I snatched, but I had only a split second to think. She won't hang up on me if he's there.'

Sandor nodded, and Jan heard her mother's voice. Not icy—cool, very cool, but definitely not icy, for presumably Donald was still within earshot. She prayed he would stay so. 'Hello, Jan. This is a late call.'

'Mother, I'm sorry—please listen. He—Sandor—is leaving here tonight.'

'Why are you telling me, darling?' The frost was there, but to anyone else listening it would seem a casual enquiry. Her mother was clever—very clever.

'Because of what you said, you know. I shall be here alone tonight, and every night.'

'I see. How interesting. Look, darling, I've got a couple of friends in for a late supper and I really can't talk, the percolator will be——'

'Please don't hang up,' Jan said desperately. Her legs felt treacherously wobbly.

'Of course not, dear,' her mother laughed. 'But I really must go—phone me in the morning.'

'What time?'

'Oh, say nine.'

'And we'll talk?'

'Oh yes, *of course* we will. 'Bye, darling.' The receiver was replaced. Jan held it for a moment longer, then put it down. Nothing had been solved—nothing. She now had the morning to anticipate, and Jan knew enough to realise she had a temporary reprieve, no more. Only because Donald was there. She turned to Sandor.

'I'll phone her in the morning.'

'What did she say?' he asked.

'Very little.'

'At least she didn't hang up on you,' he pointed out.

'Only because Donald was nearby.'

'Don't you see? If she had finished with you, she would have hung up anyway—for he would know soon enough.'

She looked at him. It was a thread of hope, a tenuous one. But Sandor was right. She nodded. 'Of course, I didn't think. It's something.'

'Come in the kitchen,' he said. 'We'll have a cup of coffee.'

'I need one.'

'And then I shall go.'

'Yes.' She walked slowly into the kitchen, and the dogs, and then Sandor, followed. He unbolted the back door and let them out while Jan put the kettle on.

Now they were alone again, and she was uneasy, remembering all that had been, and what Sandor had said. He had told her that he wanted her, but she had already known that an eternity before he had said it. Yet her treacherous mouth and body had responded. She kept a respectable distance between them while she made coffee, fetched cups, sugar, milk. As though, if she went too near, he might reach out and touch her.... He watched her, his eyes cool, giving nothing away, and there was the trace of a smile about his wide mouth, as if he guessed her thoughts. He was too dangerous.

'Thank you.' He accepted his coffee, and she went to the door to let the dogs in.

'I'll make breakfast for you in the morning. What time would you like it?'

'I shall be up at seven, no later.'

'Oh.' She looked at him, and he smiled.

'Too early? I shall take my key and let myself in quietly. I have work to do—much work, and my men arrive soon after eight.'

'And you'll work all day?' Her spirits lifted slightly. She might not see much of him at all, which was no bad thing. The better to think.

'Morning only on Saturday. And I have your car to collect as well.'

'And what do you do in the afternoon?' she asked.

'What would you like to do?'

Jan shook her head. 'No, I think it's better——' she paused.

She saw his expression change fractionally. 'If we don't see one another? Is that what you mean?'

'Something like that, yes. You know why.'

'I know several things. I know that you are confused.'

'That too,' she acknowledged dryly.

He stood up and moved, and she backed away, so that she stood against the sink. Sandor paused, frowned. 'Do I frighten you so?'

'No, of course not.' She tried a laugh, which wasn't very successful.

'Do you know, I don't believe you? You are frightened of me. Rape isn't in my vocabulary, Jan.' His voice had gone harsh. 'I am a man, with a man's needs—yes, I admit that, but I have never taken a woman by force, nor will I ever.' The last four words were said more quietly, yet they had more impact for that. She felt herself shiver, deliciously, treacherously, because she knew how he would make love; she knew it as surely as if he had already taken her, and led her along a path to ecstasy. He wouldn't need to use force. . . .

'I believe you mean what you say,' she told him.

'That is not enough.' His eyes said what his words left unsaid.

'What do you want me to add?' She lifted her chin and faced him, and the tension flowed between them, as strong as an electric current, and her heart beat rapidly. He narrowed his eyes.

'Nothing,' he said softly. He lifted up his coffee, finished it, and brought the cup over to put it on the sink beside her. 'I shall go up and get what I need for my sleep—next door. In ten minutes I shall be gone.'

'Yes,' she said. There was nothing more she could say. She wanted him to go. The rational part of her waited for him to leave. Another treacherous, secret part of her wanted him to stay. He walked quietly out of the room and she waited until she heard him going up the stairs, then began to rinse out the percolator and cups. She heard him whistling as he moved above, and for something to do, she began to set out plates and cups for the following morning's breakfast. Soon she would be alone, and then, perhaps for the first time, she would be able to think clearly. But not until. . . .

'I am ready, Jan.' Sandor deposited a sleeping bag by the door. 'And I have my key with me.'

'Then goodnight. Sleep well.'

'I shall do so. I always do. Will you?'

'I doubt it,' she answered dryly.

'Then if you have time to think, reflect on this. Reflect on whether you *really* love your fiancé, and whether you should marry him.'

He walked out, before Jan recovered the power of speech, to ask him what he meant—what on earth he could mean by such a shocking, forceful statement. The door closed. She was alone, except for the dogs, and it was past their bedtime, so that they were already looking hopefully at her to open the lounge door for them. She did so, they went in and settled down on the rug by the fireplace. Jan switched out the lights, checked that everything in the kitchen was off, and climbed the stairs.

She heard one o'clock chime, and she was more wide awake than she had been when she had gone to bed. Her mind was a confusion of thoughts and images of her life over the past year, memories of happiness and unhappiness mingled and blurred, and she opened her eyes at last in desperation and sat up in bed. She felt feverish, her head burning and aching, eyes dry, heart beating fast. Uppermost in all the confusion, the echo of Sandor's voice, insistent, 'Reflect on whether you *really* love your fiancé—reflect—reflect——'

'I do,' she said, out loud. 'I *do*!'

It was no use. She went downstairs and heated up some milk, sat in the kitchen and drank it. She was shivering now, cold instead of feverish, shocked at what she had so suddenly realised. She went over to the window and looked out at the blackness outside. Somewhere near, Sandor slept, on a floor, in a sleeping bag. And the only reason he was there was because of her. She moved away from the window restlessly, hands clenched. It was impossible, the whole situation was totally mad and utterly impossible, and—frightening. That was the most awful thing. It was frightening. You couldn't just fall out of love, especially not with the man you were going to marry in seven days, just because you had met someone else. It was impossible—but it had happened.

The pressures that had built up insidiously over the past weeks had taken their toll at last. When Jan awoke the following morning, after a nightmare-torn night, she had a raging temperature, and fell as she got out of bed. The door opening downstairs had woken her, and instinctively she got out, to make breakfast for Sandor. She didn't even reach the bedroom door. She heard him call her, but couldn't answer. The next moment she heard his steps on the stairs, then his voice again, and she tried to look up, then felt his hands round her, lifting her, then the bed beneath her again. His face swam into view as she managed to focus her eyes. A cool hand touched her forehead; she saw his frown.

'You've a temperature,' he said. 'Lie still, I'm going to get something.'

He went out, and she lay there, her body burning like fire, a raging thirst and dryness in her throat. She wondered if she were going to die, and at that moment it didn't seem to matter.

Coolness, gentle hands touching her. She moaned softly as Sandor wiped her face and neck with a damp cloth. 'I am going to fetch a doctor,' he said. 'Do you understand me?'

'Yes,' she whispered. 'But I'll be——'

'Hush, do not try to talk. You are ill.'

'No. Must phone——' her voice tailed away.

'Later. It is only past seven. There is plenty of time —later.'

'I'm—thirsty——'

'I will give you some water, that is all. Until the doctor arrives.' Soft-footed, he went out. He had covered her with the eiderdown, and she pushed it away weakly. It felt too heavy. Time passed, and drifted. It might have been minutes, or hours, before he returned and said: 'I have contacted a local doctor who will be here any time. Drink this, Jan.'

He lifted her head, and she sipped cool boiled water and pulled a face. 'Ugh!'

He smiled. 'It is safer—until the doctor comes.'

'Yes.' She lay back, he covered her again, and sat on the bed, not too near, but there. He took her hand and stroked it.

'You will soon be well,' he soothed. 'I will take care of you.'

She managed a weak smile. 'Thank you.'

'Close your eyes. Rest. I will stay with you until the doctor arrives.'

'Your work——' she began.

'No problem. That can wait.'

She must have drifted off into sleep, because she opened her eyes as the touch of his hand vanished, and she saw him going quietly out. She wanted to call after him, to tell him not to go away, because with him she was safer than she had ever been with anyone— but she couldn't make the effort to speak. Instead she waited, and listened, heard voices on the stairs, then Sandor and another man came in.

The next few minutes were a blurred memory of hands and voices, soft voices, gentle hands, then she was alone again, drifting, waiting. . . .

'He has gone.' Sandor's voice again, and she smiled at him. 'And you are to take these two tablets now.'

'I'll live?' A feeble attempt at humour, but he laughed as if she had come out with a gem of wit.

'I think so. I am *sure* so. It is a virus infection, and it has hit you harder because you are run down, but one or two days in bed will put you right. Now, these pills. The doctor will call again tomorrow.'

'He's very kind.' Jan pulled a face as she swallowed the tablets, then lay back exhausted. 'Later, I must phone my——'

'You phone no one today. I will call her. You understand?'

'But——'

Sandor put his finger on her lips. 'No arguing. The doctor has put me in complete charge of you, and you are not to move from here except for the bathroom.'

'But——' Tears sprang to Jan's eyes.

'That is an order. Now, I am going to have my breakfast. Do you feel like anything to eat? You can if you want?'

'Not yet, thank you.'

'Very well. I am going to carry you to the bathroom —will you be all right if I do? You are not to lock the door.'

'Yes.' She put up her arms as he bent down, and he lifted her as though she were a child, and carried her out of her bedroom.

Five minutes later, exhausted, she was back in bed, tucked firmly in, and Sandor left her to go down and eat, and let the dogs out. It was comforting to hear him moving about downstairs and quiet though he was, the normal everyday sounds drifted up; the clatter of plates, a door opening, the whistle of the kettle, a radio on quietly in the background. Jan wondered what time it was, whether he would be going to work soon—and it was an effort to think. It was easier to drift into a dream haze of muddled thoughts that were somehow no longer unpleasant. Jan dozed off.

When she woke again all was silent. Her aunt's bedroom clock ticked away silently on the bedside table, and the time was ten-thirty. She sat up, heart thumping with the sudden panic that filled her. He had gone— and he had forgotten to telephone, and now it would be too late—too late—— Breathless, lightheaded, she began to struggle out of the bed. Each move was a

tremendous effort; her limbs felt like lead, her head was
swimming, but she had to go downstairs to try and telephone her mother herself. . . .

She reached the door at last, and had to pause, to
wait until the room steadied before she was prepared to
tackle the stairs. It would be easier to sit on each stair,
Jan knew her balance was affected, and had no intention of falling. She reached the top, sat, and began
slowly and laboriously to make her way down. Domino
and Finn sat watching her anxiously from the hall,
whining slightly, aware that something was wrong——

'What the hell are you doing!' Sandor's voice lashed
from the door, and the next moment he had bounded
half way up the stairs to catch her arms.

'You—you frightened me!' she stammered.

'You frightened me!' he grated. 'I told you to stay
in *bed*!'

'I know, but—the phone——'

'I have already done so. Back you go. A good job I
came in to make tea——' He hefted her up and carried
her back to the bedroom, sat her on the bed, said: 'Get
in and *stay in*, I'll be back in a few minutes,' and went
out.

She shrank in, under the covers, thoroughly chast-
ened, and waited, because she had no choice. Her little
trip had taken all her strength. Ten minutes passed,
then she heard Sandor's footsteps on the stairs. He
came in carrying two beakers, put them down, and
helped her to sit up.

'You are a naughty girl,' he told her.

'Yes. I'm sorry.'

'So you should be.' Then he smiled. 'A good job I came in when I did. Here, drink your tea, and in a minute, two more pills for you. Now, I telephoned your mother at nine. I came up to tell you I was going to do so, but you were fast asleep.'

'What happened?' Jan felt as panicky and weak as she had when she had started the lone trek down the stairs.

'I told her you were ill, and the illness had been brought on by all the pressure and worry——'

'You didn't?' Her eyes were like saucers.

'I did. She was not too pleased, but she listened to me.' He smiled very gently, as if remembering. 'She—listened.'

'And——?'

'She said she might have been wrong——'

'I don't believe it!' She couldn't have kept silent at that moment for anything. Her mother was never wrong. Never. She was one of those women who had to be right, all the time, and that was that. Jan had become used to the fact years before, and managed to adjust to it. Sandor couldn't possibly have known that, and he must have heard her wrongly. That was the only acceptable explanation.

He looked surprised at the vehement tone. 'Whether you believe it or not, it is true,' he said mildly. 'She said it. She is also coming down here to talk to you.'

'When?' Jan quailed at the thought.

'Today.'

'Oh!'

'It is not what you want?'

She closed her eyes. She was no longer sure. The world was turning topsy-turvy. So many things had happened in twenty-four hours to turn life completely upside down. 'I don't know,' she admitted. 'She's a very forceful woman——'

'And I am here.'

But that wouldn't make any difference. Only she couldn't tell him. Just as she couldn't tell him that she had discovered that she no longer felt anything for Jeremy. She couldn't tell that to anyone.

'You've done enough,' she said. 'More than enough. I can't involve you in what's essentially a family matter any more. It isn't fair to you.'

'I am already involved,' he said. He looked at her, and it was as though time stood still, and she saw what was in his eyes, and was warm. 'Surely you know that?'

'Only because—because I dragged you in——' she faltered. His eyes were very steady upon her, hard, and yet not hard; with strength, and yet gentle. She began to tremble, and he put his hands on her arms and moved towards her, his hands so very strong, stronger than anything she had ever known. 'Sandor——' she began.

'Yes?' His face was only inches away, and he looked questioningly into her eyes.

'It's no use. You—we—it's better we don't——'

'Don't what? Touch each other? Because of what

might happen? Because when I touch you, we become two different people?' His voice was soft. 'Do you know what it does to me when I touch you? Is it the same for you?'

'Yes.' She barely breathed the word.

'And can you marry Jeremy, knowing that?'

'No. I'm going to tell my mother that. It will be the most difficult thing I've ever done in my life—but I have to. I know now why, and you've helped me see. But it's no use.'

'What isn't?'

'This. Us—we're attracted to each other, I know that. I'd have to be stupid not to. But it's purely physical——'

'Is that what you think, Jan?'

'Yes.' She could face him, look directly into those grey eyes that saw into her soul. 'Yes, it must be. You can't just fall out of love with one man and straight in love with another——'

'Were you ever in love with him?'

She was silent, and in that silence Sandor drew her to him and kissed her. In a brief moment of protest, Jan said weakly: 'You'll catch——'

'I'll catch nothing——' he said, then they were both silent as their mouths met in a wild hunger that left no room for anything else. Jan reached for him with a strength she didn't know she possessed, and clung to him as he caressed and kissed her with a mounting excitement, a frenzy of ecstasy that left them both shattered.

He drew away after timeless minutes and looked at her. 'I want you now,' he said. 'I want you so much that nothing else matters.' His voice was deep and harsh, and his hand shook as he reached to stroke her face. 'Dear God, how I want you—as I've never wanted any woman before.'

She too was trembling in the aftermath of his love-making, her body afire with the fever for him, and she closed her eyes because she could not bear the pain in him, the ache that she shared. 'But we will wait,' he said, 'until your mother has been. Until it is—official, then——'

'And then?' she questioned softly, knowing already.

'And then I will ask you to be my wife,' he said quietly. Both his hands were on her face now, gently touching, a butterfly caress. 'For I love you, and I want you——'

'I love you,' she whispered. 'I think I've loved you since the first few minutes I saw you.'

'When we were fighting?' he teased.

'Even then.'

'And that is why we must both be strong. Jeremy is not your lover, is he?'

'No.'

'Ah.' He sighed. 'I knew. I knew when I saw him that he had not——' he paused.

'How did you know?'

He shrugged. 'I did, that was all. You were meant for me. Does that sound conceited?'

'No.' Jan knew it to be true. 'I knew it too. Do you

know something? I feel better! I feel hungry too.'

Sandor started to laugh. 'Then you shall eat. I will go and prepare something now.'

'What about your men?'

He looked surprised. 'They are working. They can manage.' He grinned. 'Stay there in bed. I like to see you in bed. Then you will eat, and we will decide what we are going to say to my future mother-in-law.' He stood up. All fear rolled away from Jan. Had she ever been frightened of Jeremy, of her mother? Had she really? It didn't seem possible. She began to laugh softly.

'Don't be long,' she said. 'We've a lot to plan.'

He looked at her. 'Yes.' Then he went quietly out. Jan lay back and basked in a warm glow of love. She was mad. They were both mad, but it was a madness she wouldn't change for anything in the world. She loved; she was loved. The shallowness of her relationship with Jeremy was all the more starkly outlined with the contrast of what she now knew. She closed her eyes, and saw Sandor's face in her mind, filling her very being. She knew what happiness was now.

He brought up scrambled egg on toast, and it was a feast fit for the gods because he had made it. Jan ate it hungrily and then said: 'I'm getting up now.'

'No, you're not.' She looked at him defiantly.

'Yes, I am. You've cured me. Anyway, I'm not safe in bed with you around.'

'True.' He sighed. 'Very well, but slowly. Do you want any help?'

'Do you think I'd ever get dressed with you helping me?'

He frowned as if considering the question. 'No,' he admitted, after some moments' thought. 'But it could be more fun.'

'Very true. The only trouble is, my mother might well arrive at the wrong moment. We don't want to upset her more than necessary, do we?'

'No, you have a point there. Very well, I shall leave you now. Take your time, Jan. You are very precious to me.' He smiled and went out of the room, leaving her alone.

She swung her feet carefully over the side, tested them on the floor, and was only mildly surprised to find she had almost as much strength as normal. In a day she would be well again, fully recovered, she knew that now. And all because of Sandor....

Slowly she began to get dressed. Then she took off her engagement ring for the last time and left it on the dressing table to give to her mother to return to Jeremy.

She walked very carefully and slowly down the stairs, and Sandor came into the hall and lifted her down the last step. 'Into the lounge,' he said, 'and we will talk.' His arm round her was where it belonged, as if this had been meant from long ago, as if there had never been a time when they had not been in each other's lives. She turned to him in the lounge and told him so, and he answered that he knew it too, and kissed her.

Then, when they were sitting down, he began to talk, and Jan listened.

When her mother arrived they were ready and waiting for her—together.

CHAPTER SIX

CORAL HUNTER made a grand entrance, as she always did. The only thing that marred it was the fact that there was no one there to greet her as she arrived and she had to walk through the front door, crying: 'Jan, where are you?'

There was a silence following. Then, from the kitchen, Sandor walked into the hall and looked at Jan's mother. Jan, sitting in the kitchen, waited, heart in mouth, for what would happen next. This was unthinkable! Normally, on hearing the three imperious toots on her mother's car horn, she would have rushed to the door. Sandor had already elicited that fact from her, and when the horn blasts came, touched her arm. 'Wait,' he said. 'It is important. Wait.'

She knew he was right. It took a tremendous effort to sit there not moving, holding the dogs. Then Sandor stood, went into the hall, and Jan heard him say through the closed door, 'Good afternoon, Mrs Hunter, please come in.'

Her heart thudded so fast she thought she might not hear her mother's reply, but she did. Coral Hunter had a splendid carrying voice. '*Where* is *my* daughter?' It carried ice in it as well.

'In the kitchen, holding the dogs so that they would not rush out.'

'I thought you said she was ill?'

'She was. Do come in.' The door opened, Jan released the dogs, who rushed to greet the newcomer, and walked towards her mother.

'Hello, Mother,' she said, and went to kiss her mother's cheek. Coral Hunter stepped back as if threatened, and Jan hesitated. The move was like a slap in the face.

'I don't want to catch anything, dear,' her mother explained.

'It's not catching, merely exhaustion.' Sandor had seen, yet his voice held no expression save politeness. Coral Hunter turned to him.

'I'd like to speak to my daughter—alone,' she said. Hers was the voice that gave the orders that were passed down to thousands of employees, and nobody, but nobody, ever disagreed with her, nor had done so for years.

'He can stay,' said Jan. 'I want him to.' She caught Sandor's eye and he winked at her. That was enough.

'Don't be stupid, darling.' Her mother's eyes narrowed, and Jan, looking at her clearly, saw that she was seeing a stranger. Her mother was as beautiful as ever, no doubt about that, with her auburn hair swept back, and up, into a neat chignon, with her pale sculpted features, the good cheekbones accentuated by the merest whisper of pale blusher, the gorgeous dark eyes and thick eyebrows, and the shapely mouth—but it was a stranger speaking. Coral put her handbag and gloves down on the table.

'I'd like a coffee. I've had a very long drive,' she said,

and sat down. Sandor went over to fill the kettle, and Jan sat opposite her mother who, ignoring Jan completely, began to look in her bag. She produced her gold cigarette case and lighter, lit herself a cigarette and sat there. This was the cat and mouse stage, and Jan had told Sandor what would happen. She felt surprised at how accurately her mother's actions could be assessed, and found herself watching her. It wasn't only her mother who could play the game, Sandor had said. Three could join in. Coral's eyes were on her. Hard, dark blue eyes, very shrewd. Silence. The only sounds in the kitchen were the plop of the gas, the growing shrillness of the kettle, and Sandor putting ground coffee in the pot.

Jan stood up and went over for beakers, milk and sugar. She stole a glance at the man she loved, fearful that something would go wrong, and saw the expression on his face, and knew quite suddenly that at last her mother had met her match. Sandor would be a match for anyone. The dogs had retired into the lounge. After greeting Coral they had wandered out.

Sandor put an ashtray on the kitchen table, then turned away to fill the percolator. Coral spoke. 'All right,' she said. 'What's going on?'

'What do you mean?' Jan asked.

Coral arched one eyebrow. Her mouth twisted. 'Don't try and take me for a fool, darling,' she answered. 'I've been at this game a while longer than you. All right, Mr Gregas, I imagine you've a few things to say. Your back is very expressive, you know.'

He turned and grinned at her. 'Is it? You are right, I have many things to say—but first, the coffee. You have, as you say, driven a long way. One must observe the social niceties. Milk?'

'Black.' She snapped her handbag shut. 'I don't know what you're up to, but I can tell you our conversation this morning didn't please me. That's partly why I came down—also because you gave me the strong impression that Jan was in bed suffering from exhaustion——'

'She was. She is much better now, since she and I talked. Jan, coffee for you?'

'Please.'

He began to pour into the beakers; Coral watched him. Jan didn't like the expression on her mother's face. 'I have several things to say to you,' said Coral. 'I don't like you being here for a start, but then Jessie always was a fool—and I don't like you, from what I've heard, and now seen—and I am not much impressed by the fact that you're supposed to be sleeping in that house next door—it isn't even built yet——'

'Nevertheless that is where I spent the night,' he cut in.

She went on as if he hadn't spoken. 'My daughter is getting married next week, and I've come here to persuade her to come home with me. The reason I wanted to speak to her alone is that I don't intend to let you interfere. For some reason, I feel, she's being foolishly influenced by you. God knows why, but there it is. She always was easily led.' She smiled contemptuously at

Jan, then looked back at Sandor, who had remained standing by the cooker, holding his coffee.

'As we are speaking frankly, Mrs Hunter,' he said, 'perhaps you will forgive me for being equally frank. The fact that you don't like me is, quite honestly, not something I care about one way or the other. You are entitled to your opinions, and if Jan herself wishes me to leave the room I shall do so. But after seeing Jeremy's treatment of her, I am most reluctant. He is a bully—as you are. She should be able to deal with that fact, for I'm sure she is well used to it, but I don't like to see anyone bullied——'

'How dare you!' Two spots of colour burned on her mother's face. 'You're insufferably rude!'

'I speak what I see. That is what I see—it is you who believes in frank speaking—as long, apparently, as you are the only one doing it. You don't frighten me—and you don't frighten Jan. Having said that, why don't you accept that she intends to stay here, and let it go at that?'

Jan spoke then. 'I *am* staying here,' she said quietly. 'I'm sorry if you've had a wasted journey.'

'You're *not*! Not now.'

'Mother, I'm not going to marry Jeremy.'

Coral jumped to her feet. 'My God! You're quite *mad*!' she shrieked, all her superb self-control vanished in an instant. She turned on Sandor. 'What have you done?' she demanded. Her eyes glittered with overpowering rage, and she looked as though she would kill him if she could. Jan got to her feet.

'He's done nothing,' she said. 'But he's made me see——'

'See? See what? Him? A foreigner?' Coral moved towards him. 'Get out of this room. Get *out*!' She was trembling with anger. Jan had never seen her in such a state. She faced the calm man who stood there looking at her almost with pity in his eyes. 'Get out at once. I'll deal with my daughter now—I'll deal with you afterwards.'

'Deal? Who do you think you are?' he asked.

'I'll tell you who I am, you—you *peasant*!' she hissed. 'I'm Jan's *mother*, and this concerns the two of us, not *you*. Not a stranger like you, who thinks he knows all the answers. I know a few more than you, *boy*—I've made it my business to. Does that surprise you, eh? I came down here armed with a few weapons you can't even guess about—oh yes, Mr Gregas, you'll know who I am all right, in a minute. I made it my business to do some checking up on you. Does that surprise you?'

'No,' he said. 'I would have expected it. Tell me, what did you find out?'

'Plenty,' she snapped. 'More than enough. I've checked up on your business, your associates, your *friends*——' she laughed in his face. 'I have friends of my own, who're only too willing to oblige me.'

'I'll bet you have.' He nodded. Then he smiled. Coral, incensed, struck out at him and caught him a stinging slap on his face.

Jan froze, went numb. She saw his expression

change, but he didn't move.

'Thank you,' he said. 'I hope that made you feel better. At least you didn't hit Jan.'

'Damn you!' She whirled round on Jan. 'Has he told you why he's leaving London? I'll bet he's not. It's because the place is too hot for him. Several women have made it so—no, I can see he didn't tell you *that*. It's a wonder he's not persuaded you into bed yet—although I'm not too sure about that, looking at you; he's had remarkable success with all the others. In fact he's got quite a reputation as a ladies' man.' She turned back to face him, leaving Jan, mercifully, alone. 'What? Not denying it?'

'There would be no point.' His voice was as expressionless as his face. 'I'm quite sure your friends think they know it all, but they don't. Nor do you. You might be better employed checking up on John Redmayne—Jeremy's father—and the money he owes all round. Money is a more important concern to you than my affairs, I'm quite sure. I have done work for him in my business—though I'm sure I'm not telling you anything you don't know. What your informants may have failed to find out is precisely how rocky his business is. But then he keeps that a close secret.'

There was a brief stunned silence. 'I'd be careful what I said if I were you,' said Coral in dangerous tones. But her eyes had gone wary.

'But you're not me,' Sandor remarked. 'And I shall say what I choose. John Redmayne is as near bankrupt as makes no difference. Only his family name and influential friends have kept him going so far——'

'You liar!' she spat out.

'Madam, I am not a liar.' His voice was whiplash, cutting now, and he looked dangerous. 'I can prove the truth of what I say. Which is more than you can do with your slanderous remarks about me. Moreover, and I'm sure this has been kept from you, he was involved in a very unsavoury land deal a short time ago. If that gets out—and it surely will—your name, as his son's mother-in-law, could be dragged in, which wouldn't do your social standing much good.' Coral sat down suddenly as if her legs would no longer support her. She was ashen-faced. Sandor looked at her again with something approaching pity in his eyes, then at Jan.

'I'm sorry, Jan,' he said. 'I had no intention of telling you this way.'

'You knew *that*?' she whispered.

'Yes, it is true. I am sorry.'

'My God!' Coral closed her eyes. 'This is terrible!'

'Yes, it is,' he agreed. 'But you don't need to worry. Jan isn't going to marry Jeremy. She is going to marry me.'

Coral looked up at him, then at Jan. She was dazed. 'What did he say?' she said, in a broken voice.

'Sandor has asked me to marry him,' said Jan gently, 'and I've said yes.'

Coral put her hand to her face. 'No,' she whispered. 'No!'

'Yes,' said Sandor. 'I had better get you a drink. I feel

you need one.' He went out of the room. Coral looked up at Jan. Tears filled her eyes, and Jan knew why she had seen the look of pity in Sandor's eyes. This was a different woman from the one who had entered the house so recently.

'This will ruin me,' she muttered.

'It won't. I don't love Jeremy——'

'Not that. The scandal—the wedding cancelled—what will everyone say?'

Jan could scarcely believe her ears. Was that all that concerned her mother? What people would say? She felt an intense surge of pity for her mother herself. What a life it must be, to live by other people's opinions. Sandor's statement about Jeremy's father had shocked her terribly—but not as much as it had shocked her mother. And now she knew why.

He came in with a bottle of brandy, found a glass, and poured some in. 'Drink that,' he said, handing Coral the glass. She took it, sipped, then swallowed the contents in one gulp. Some of the colour came back. 'You had better stay a while,' he went on. 'You are in no condition to drive back to London yet.' Subtly he had taken charge. 'There is room for you to stay the night if you wish. You can have my old bedroom.' This with a dry irony that wasn't lost on either woman.

Coral looked up at him. She was a fighter. 'Why do *you* want to marry my daughter?' she asked.

'What would you like me to say? For her money?' He placed his hands flat on the table, palms down, arms straight, and stared levelly at Coral Hunter. 'Be-

cause I don't intend to—although I don't expect *you*
to believe me. I am well aware of how wealthy you are,
as I'm sure is everyone in London, but as my wife, Jan
will be supported by *me*. And I'm sure you've done
your homework on that matter better than you have
on my personal habits. I could certainly buy and sell
John and Jeremy Redmayne.' He seemed to be choos-
ing his words for maximum effect. Jan felt she was seeing a different man from the one she thought she had
known. Coral sat very still, as if to move would be too
great an effort.

'And now I'm going to take the dogs out so that you
can talk. I don't go when I'm ordered to. I go because
I choose.' He went out, calling the dogs from out of the
lounge as he did so.

He left a silence behind him. Jan was the first to
break it. 'Don't expect me to apologise for the way he
spoke to you,' she said, 'because I'm not going to.'

Coral looked at her. She had aged visibly in the last
few minutes. 'I never knew you had it in you,' she said
flatly.

'Perhaps you didn't know me very well,' Jan an-
swered gently. 'Oh, Mother——' her voice broke.
Coral did an unexpected thing. She put her hand over
Jan's.

'Don't,' she said. 'Don't cry any more. I can't
take——' she too stopped. 'I think I need another
drink.' She poured some more brandy in the glass. 'He
was speaking the truth, wasn't he?'

'How could he have made it up?'

'Oh God, what am I going to do? I knew—I've known for a while—I've sensed all wasn't well with the Redmaynes, but it seemed important for everything to be all right. No wonder——' Coral stopped.

'No wonder what?' prompted Jan.

'No wonder Jeremy was in such a hurry for you to get married!'

'Is that all you can think about—money?' Jan burst out.

Coral looked at her. 'What else is there?' she said bitterly. 'You'll find out, when you're older. Where's the phone?'

'In the hall. Who——'

'Who do you think? I'm going to have a talk with John Redmayne——'

'Wait,' said Jan. 'Not yet.'

'Why?' her mother demanded. 'I'll say what I've got to say. It won't change for waiting.'

'I've got to speak to Jeremy first. It's only fair——'

'Fair? I've finished being fair,' her mother snapped. You never were, thought Jan, but said nothing. Her mother took her glass with her, and Jan heard her dialling. She didn't want to listen, but she was going to have to. She felt tired and ill again, and wanted nothing so much as to lie down and sleep. But things had gone too far for that. Much too far. . . .

The conversation was brief, bitter, and to the point. Jan heard Coral slam the receiver down, and winced.

'That's it.' Coral glared at her. 'They're coming down.'

'Oh no!' Horror-struck, Jan stared at her in disbelief.

'Oh yes. In the helicopter—they'll be here in an hour or less. John was nearly incoherent.'

'I heard you. I'm not surprised.'

Coral smiled thinly. 'I don't see why I should be the only one to suffer.'

'Suffer? You?' Jan smiled at that, then sobered. It wasn't funny; none of it was. It was the most awful thing that had ever happened, a nightmare, and growing worse with every twist and turn—and she couldn't imagine where it could all end. Only one thing stood out above it all. Sandor. She loved him, and he loved her. And nothing was going to spoil that. Nothing.

It was evening. Once more the house was quiet, but only after the most action-packed, *awful* afternoon of Jan's life. It had been a terrible ordeal, but now the ordeal was over, for good. She was no longer engaged to Jeremy. There had been a terrible scene with him in which she had seen another side, an unimaginable side to his character which would have decided her if nothing else had. She had seen a petty, vicious streak in him that had shocked and sickened her.

The only person to emerge apparently unscathed was Sandor. There was no time at which he had lost control at all. And now, as Jan sat, drained, in the lounge, he came in and sat beside her. 'It is all over,' he said. 'All over. We are alone, just you and I.'

'Thank the lord for that,' she murmured, and took

his hand. 'I never want to live through anything like that again!'

'It's an early night for you tonight,' he said, and kissed her. 'You are not well yet. There are many tomorrows for us, just remember that, and we will be married as soon as I can see about getting a licence.'

'Yes,' she said. 'Oh yes!' She closed her eyes and lay back in the shelter of his arms, which was the only place she wanted to be, and he turned, to hold her more comfortably, then his mouth came down on hers, warm, gentle yet demanding, with the promise of excitement stirring in them both. No words were needed any more.

Huskily he spoke, after timeless minutes or hours. 'No,' he said. 'We must be strong. When I make love to you we will be married.'

'Mmm,' she said, and laughing, caught hold of him. 'If you say so.'

'Witch!' he growled. 'Leave me alone——'

'No. Come here.'

'Unhand me, madam,' he whispered, 'or I shall not be responsible for the consequences.'

'Mmm, lovely!'

Then they were both laughing, secretly, like lovers the world over, he pretending to fight her off, not quite succeeding, not caring. Outside it grew dark, and darker, and he said firmly, eventually: 'That's *enough*. You'll be falling asleep any minute—and that would damage my pride more than anything else.' He laughed at her tired face, and kissed her nose. It was the ideal moment to ask him what her mother had meant about his other women. It had been a mere thought at the very back of Jan's mind all afternoon, no more, in the face of all the other things going on. But she didn't want to spoil the warm perfection of the moment, and the question died unasked. She should have asked it.

Later she lay in bed after her two final tablets of the day, absolutely exhausted, and resolutely put everything out of her mind. There was work to be done on Monday, in London, but she had the weekend with Sandor, just the two of them before that.

On Monday the announcement would be in the papers. 'The marriage arranged between Mr Jeremy Redmayne and Miss Janette Hunter will not now take place. . . .' A bald statement that would cause a furore, and she had to be there. This time she wasn't going to run away. She had done it once, she would never do it again. She didn't need to.

There were presents to be returned, telephone calls to be made, cables to be sent—and very possibly reporters to be avoided. In a week or so she would marry Sandor, very quietly, and they would slip away together for a few days, that was all, somewhere peaceful, then live in the house that he was building when it was done. Jan had telephoned her Aunt Jessie that evening and broken the news to her. Her reaction had been typical. She had not sounded a scrap surprised. She was coming home Sunday afternoon, because there was hardly any point in her remaining in London for a wedding that would not now take place.

Jan smiled to herself, turned over, and fell asleep. She dreamed of Sandor.

Sunday. A very distant peal of bells woke Jan, who lay there pleasantly on the threshold of sleep for a few moments before remembering where she was. She stretched, yawned, and felt splendid. She felt better than she had for months. She wondered where Sandor was, if he was still asleep, or up, and she wondered, but only vaguely, what time it was. It was too much effort to look at the clock. . . . But she ought to get up and make breakfast. Today would probably be the last quiet day for some time. Tomorrow would be hectic—but she didn't want to think about that, not until it was necessary. She rolled back the covers and got out of bed, fumbling for her dressing gown and slippers. Then she went very quietly down, so as not to wake him. She intended to surprise him with breakfast in bed.

There was a note on the kitchen table, and there were no dogs waiting to greet her. 'Darling,' it said, 'I have gone to buy Sunday papers and I have borrowed your car. The dogs are with me, Sandor.' Jan liked his writing. She had never seen it before. Dark strong strokes, very firm and decisive—something like him, in fact. She smiled and put the note down, then began to prepare the breakfast for them both. It looked as though she was going to have a husband who was an early riser. She pulled a face, laughed about that, and put on the kettle. Someone was going to have to be trained, and she had a feeling it wouldn't be him.

The bacon was sizzling gently under the grill when the front door opened and the dogs burst into the kitchen, nearly knocking her over in the enthusiasm of their greeting. Sandor followed, smelling of fresh sea air, gloriously unshaven, and kissed her.

'How are you, my darling?' he asked. Jan rubbed her face and winced.

'Ouch! I was fine until you kissed me,' she grumbled, hiding a smile.

He laughed and pinched her cheek. 'You will learn to put up with it. I shall go and shave now. One egg only for me, please—and two pieces of toast.' He laid a pile of Sunday papers on the table, slapped her bottom, and went out.

'Yes, oh master,' she called after him, and heard him laugh as he ran up the stairs.

It was perfect. She thought she must surely die of happiness. Just to be there, with him, the two of them together, alone in the cottage, was a bliss she could never have imagined in a thousand years. The love welled up in her, and she wanted to run after him and tell him she loved him more than anything in the world, because he ought to know—but she didn't, because the bacon was nearly ready, and the toaster about to pop up, and because there was also all the time in the world for it to be told, later.

They ate together, reading the papers, just like an old married couple, pointing out pieces of interest, sharing the laughter, sharing their breakfast with the dogs, who were enjoying themselves no end, and the time passed on wings. Sandor went to work in the lounge afterwards, and Jan vacuumed and dusted the house ready for her aunt's return that afternoon. She was looking forward to seeing Aunt Jessie again—to telling her the full story, slightly censored, of course, for there was no point in distressing her unnecessarily. She would understand, she always did.

She took Sandor a cup of coffee in at one, and he kissed her hand as he thanked her. 'I shall soon be finished,' he said. Papers were spread out on the table in glorious confusion.

'Can I help you?' Jan asked.

'No, thank you. All goes well. I know exactly where I am up to. You would only distract me.' She leaned over him and put her arms round his neck.

'I don't see how,' she complained.

He laughed. 'I do. Your perfume is a distraction to start with. Go *away*!' This in mock severe tones. She pulled a face at him.

'You're a beast,' she muttered. His mouth twitched.

'You will see what sort of beast I am in a minute if you don't leave me—and then I shall have no more work done at all.' He stood up suddenly and turned round to face her, grabbed hold of her and began to kiss her. It started as a joke, she pretending to struggle, to try and escape—and then suddenly it wasn't a joke any more, and they stood locked in each other's arms, lost to the world, their bodies on fire with the nearness, Sandor whispering: 'I do love you so very much, my dearest. Oh, how I love you, Jan.'

'I know. You don't need to say it,' she murmured. 'I love you very much too.' They kissed, and time ceased to have any meaning any more—then they heard a car horn outside and broke apart quickly, he laughing, she with pink cheeks.

'It's Aunt Jessie!' she whispered. 'Oops!'

'You minx! I've got to appear calm to welcome her, and I'm a trembling wreck. Just you wait!' he threatened, and tried vainly to straighten his hair, as they walked towards the door to welcome Aunt Jessie home.

Aunt Jessie was the soul of tact. She didn't immediately appear, and presumably had tooted the car horn in fair warning, which gave them time to open the front door, to see her waving from her mini as she struggled to open the boot.

'Hello, my dears,' she called. 'I do hope the kettle's on.' Sandor went down to help her, and Jan followed. She ran the last few steps to hug her plump elderly aunt while Sandor opened the boot.

'Oh, it's good to see you, love,' Aunt Jessie smiled. 'And there's so much to talk about—and so many questions. First things first, though. I want a cup of tea.' She raised her face as Sandor put down her case, then bent to kiss her cheek.

'Hello, Miss Ingles,' he said, 'and thank you.'

'What for, dear?' Jessie looked puzzled.

'For having a niece like Jan.' He picked up her case, put his arm round her, and, laughing, the three of them went back into the cottage.

CHAPTER SEVEN

THEY did all their talking that afternoon, and after tea, when they were sitting by a warm fire in the lounge, for the evening was going chilly, Aunt Jessie came out with her piece of news.

'I've an idea,' she said, 'but it's only a suggestion, you understand. Would you like to live here in this cottage after you're married, until your house is completed?'

Sandor and Jan looked at one another, and Aunt Jessie went on: 'Not with me! Heavens, no—only Dolly has been trying to persuade me to go on a long cruise for ages, and I've always had to turn it down, because of the dogs, you see. But if you wouldn't mind——' She looked wistfully at them, and Jan burst out laughing.

'I can't imagine anything more perfect, can you, Sandor?'

He smiled. 'It would solve a lot of problems. But are you sure——'

'I'm positive, my dears,' Aunt Jessie said firmly. 'When will your house be finished?'

'A few more weeks, really, that's all. It would be ideal, Miss Ingles.'

'Hadn't you better call me Aunt Jessie?'

'Aunt Jessie—thank you. Jan and I would be very happy to accept your kind offer.' Sandor stood up, went

111

over and kissed her. 'For that I think we shall have a drink to celebrate. What will it be?'

'Oh, sherry for me, dear. Then I'll have an early night, I think. That drive from London is quite tiring. I'll go and phone Dolly first, and tell her the good news.' Sandor helped her to her feet and she trotted out.

Jan went and hugged him. 'Isn't that terrific!'

'It is.' He lifted her off her feet, hugging her tightly. 'I can think of nowhere else I would rather be with you than here.' They kissed.

'Sandor.' She looked up at him. 'You know I must go back to London tomorrow.'

'Yes, I know.' His face was serious. 'But only for a day or two. I cannot be away from you longer than that.'

'I can't bear it either. But there are lots of things—not very pleasant things to do, and it must be me who does them.'

'Yes, you must. I will phone you very often, never fear,' he smiled down at her. 'Cheer up, all will be well.'

'Yes,' she smiled.

'Shall I come with you? Would you like that?'

'You know I would. But you have your work down here—and my mother'—she pulled a face—'isn't the easiest person to get on with.'

'That I do know. But she and I understand each other.'

'I think you *do*!' She looked at him. 'You know, you're right. She was different when she'd been here a while, and it was you——' she blinked. 'Good grief!

I've never seen anyone talk to her like you did before.'

'It was necessary. I was hard—I am aware of that. I did not choose to be so, it was forced on me.'

'I know. And you were right, of course. Who knows, with any luck, she might actually welcome you as a son-in-law——' Jan stopped as her aunt came in beaming.

'There, that's settled. Er—you said something about sherry?'

'Forgive me.' Sandor released Jan and went out of the room. Aunt Jessie smiled.

'He's a lovely man,' she said. 'I thought, when I first met him——' she stopped guiltily.

'You thought what?' demanded Jan. But she had a strange feeling that she already knew.

'Nothing, dear.' Aunt Jessie smiled vaguely and turned towards the door. 'Ah, the barman returns. Do you know, I'm really looking forward to a drop of sherry? Sandor is so kind, he bought several bottles of drink——' She burbled on, but Jan didn't listen. What would her aunt have thought? That she and Sandor were ideal for one another? She smiled secretly to herself, hugging the knowledge. How perfect everything was. Perfect. And always would be.

She was to remember that thought, and that moment of time in which the world stretched ahead in a golden haze, when not too many weeks had passed, but then, at that moment, she had no foreknowledge of what was to come.

She and Sandor were married very quietly two weeks later in the small church ten miles away from Aunt Jessie's house, the bells of which Jan had heard that first Sunday morning of knowing Sandor. Aunt Jessie and her friend Dolly were the only guests and witnesses, and immediately after the wedding were to depart on their cruise from Southampton.

Sandor drove Jan back to the cottage and carried her over the threshold, puzzling the dogs mightily in the process. He put her down in the hall and kissed her. 'Welcome to your honeymoon home, Mrs Gregas,' he said.

'Thank you, Mr Gregas,' she murmured. 'Shall I fetch the champagne from the fridge?'

'Why not? Then we'll have an early night.'

'But it's only four-thirty——' She stopped.

'Mmm. As I said—an early night.' He looked at her, and she saw what was in his eyes, and a warmth spread through her. 'On second thoughts,' he added, 'I think the champagne could cool a while longer.' He caught hold of her and began to undo the buttons of her long blue dress.

She caught his hand. 'Please, sir—not here!'

'Then,' he said huskily, 'you'd better walk up the stairs. Or do you want me to carry you?'

'Yes,' she whispered. He picked her up and carried her up the stairs and into the bedroom. He set her down and closed the door, bent his head and kissed her neck, and his hands were warm upon her waiting body. She melted into his warmth, feeling the hard length of him against her. Then he undressed her slowly, taking infinite care in the process, until she wanted to cry out for him to take her—and he knew, all right—he knew precisely what he was doing, and he revelled in it.

'Sandor, for God's sake,' she whispered, when she could bear it no more, and she bit his ear. He winced, then began to laugh softly.

'You'll pay for that,' he growled—then suddenly he was no longer laughing, nor was she. He picked her up and carried her over to the bed; they fell upon it together in a tangle of limbs, and now there was an urgency in him that more than matched her own. She cried out something, she knew not what, in her ecstasy and desire, then caught him and held him, and they made love in a raging torrent of passion that caught them and carried them along beyond all reason or thinking. . . .

They slept for a short while, exhausted, and Jan awoke to see Sandor bending over her, his face very near, his eyes so full of love for her that she thought she would die of happiness. He murmured huskily: 'Oh, Mrs Gregas, how you surprise me,' and bent to kiss her. The excitement began again, and this time, now, there was no haste or urgency, but a gentleness that was even more perfect than the first time had been. It was dark before they eventually made their way downstairs for the champagne that they had planned to drink hours and hours before.

The barking of the dogs, asking to be let out, awoke Jan

the following morning, and she sat up, fumbling for her dressing gown, and saw to her horror that it was nearly noon. She began to laugh, and prodded the sleeping man by her side.

'Wake up, Sandor. Do you know what time it is?'

'No. And I don't care,' he murmured sleepily.

'It's nearly twelve—I'm going out to let the poor dogs out.'

'Mmm? Good.' He turned over and pulled the covers round him more firmly. She sighed, and looked at him, pulled on her dressing gown, and went down the stairs.

As she sat in the kitchen drinking her hot coffee, waiting for the dogs to return, she studied her brand new wedding ring. It was a simple, thick gold band, and Sandor wore its twin—slightly larger, of course. It was quite perfect. Jan held her left hand away from her, the better to see it. She had refused to allow Sandor to buy her an engagement ring. It hadn't seemed important, and did not now. There were other, far more important things in life, and most important of all was the fact that she had married the man she loved. The only man she had ever loved, she realised now.

She sighed happily and went to turn the bacon over under the grill. Sandor was going to have breakfast—a very late breakfast—in bed. Later that afternoon they were going to plan the furnishing of their new, nearly completed house next door.

Tomorrow he would be back at work on it. Both had agreed that the honeymoon proper could come later, when the house was done. They would fly to America to visit relatives of his, a sister, some cousins. Jan stood at the cooker and thought about it. She knew very little about the man she had married—not that it mattered, she knew all she wanted to know. Yet he talked little of his family. She sensed some pain in his life, and had tactfully avoided the subject. When he was ready, when he wanted to talk, that would be the time. She already knew that he was strong, forceful, and totally honest. This was something she had sensed about him all along. He had a direct way of speaking, of expressing himself, that appealed to her own innate honesty. He made everything appear so simple and straightforward. It was probably that facet of his character that had enabled him to cope so beautifully with her mother.

They had an invitation to go and stay there any time they wished, which was a major triumph in itself. Normally her mother was inflexible, and totally committed to her own point of view. With Sandor, she had changed. The hurt of the broken engagement, especially so soon before the wedding, was not an easy thing to get over, yet it seemed as if Coral Hunter had already come to terms with it. Jan hoped that when they did visit, everything would go perfectly.

The bacon and eggs were done, the toast was buttered, and she put everything on a tray and took it upstairs.

Later that day they made all their plans for their future life in the new house nearby, spent a quiet evening watching television and had an early night.

It wasn't until the next morning that everything started to go horribly wrong.

Jan had dusted and tidied the cottage, received a not unpleasant telephone call from her mother—strange, she thought, at one point during their conversation, how she doesn't really upset me any more—and was making herself a cup of tea, when she heard an engine outside, followed moments later by a rap on the front door.

She turned the kettle off and went to answer it. A postman stood there with a parcel and several letters. 'Gregas?' he said.

'Yes.'

'Sign here, please—registered parcel, and some letters.'

He handed her a notebook, indicated where she was to sign, and waited patiently while she did so. Then he handed her the letters and parcel, and with a cheery good morning departed.

The parcel was for her, as was one of the letters. The rest were for Aunt Jessie. Jan carried them all through to the kitchen and opened the large soft packet. It was a wedding present from a close friend, Marianne, a beautiful lace bedcover. It had a brief note to say that Marianne had only just heard of her wedding—and was delighted, and that a more detailed letter would follow. Jan smiled to herself. Marianne knew everyone and everything—her letter would be full of comment about what London was saying about Jan's defection. She and Jan were close enough to speak freely about anything under the sun. Jan decided that she would telephone later in the day, and perhaps invite Marianne down to visit. She opened the envelope, still smiling about the talk they would have later, and began to read the letter. Only it wasn't to her, it was to Sandor. But by the time she realised that fact it was too late to stop reading. Much too late.

She sat down very carefully, because the room had started to tilt dangerously, and she was no longer sure if she could stand up. The letter was very clear, much too clear, and it shattered Jan's world into tiny fragments. She counted to ten, very slowly, then began to read it again, just in case, by some miracle, the meaning might have changed. But it hadn't. 'Dear Sandor,' she read, 'Thank you for the monthly cheque which arrived safely last week. I'm sorry I didn't write before, but Nicky is just getting over the chickenpox, and it's been a busy time. He's nearly four now, and keeps asking after you. Please come and visit us soon—I know it's difficult for you, being so busy, but Nicky needs a father. We're on the phone now. Please ring, I have something important to tell you. Love, Alison.'

The writing was carefully formed, almost childish. Jan felt sick. She looked again at the address, which was in a village a mere fifteen miles away. Was this why Sandor had moved here, to be near his child? Had he intended to have Nicky and Alison with him—until he met Jan? She rubbed her forehead, to still the throbbing in her temples. He paid each month for the child's upkeep—but then he could well afford to. It would be nothing to him. What was it her mother had said, in that first fine rush of temper, after striking him? She tried desperately to remember. London was too hot for him, she had said, because of women—with whom he had remarkable success. And this girl didn't even live in London. How many more were there? How many children being paid for? How old was she? Somehow that seemed important. The writing was so young, as though Alison were scarcely more than a child herself. And she had Sandor's four-year-old son. But he had said not a word about it.

The tea could wait, as could everything else. Jan knew what she was going to do. She had to see for herself, had to know, to see his ex-mistress. Or maybe it had only been a casual fling, soon regretted. Which was worse, she did not know.

She picked up her bag and keys, left the dogs in the lounge, and went out to her car. She would have to drive past Sandor, working, and she prayed he would not wave to her, to ask where she was going, because at that moment she didn't feel that she could speak to him ever again.

He was nowhere to be seen, although one of his workmen was attending to the churning cement mixer, and gave her a cheery salute as she drove past. She had the letter in her bag. She had no plans as to what she would say. But nothing would have stopped her going. Nothing.

The cottage was at the far end of the village, and Jan stopped a way past it and walked back, heart in mouth, towards the gate. A young boy was playing with an old tyre in the garden, and he looked up at Jan's approach and grinned.

'Hello,' he said. She stopped, clutching to the gate for support. He was the image of Sandor. If there had been a mistake—if—she had clung to some vague hope that it might have all been a dream, with a rational explanation—this shattered it. There was no mistaking those features, young though the child was.

'Can I help you?' The cottage door had opened, and a girl stood there. Two things registered simultaneously with Jan. The first—she was scarcely more than twenty. The next—she was pregnant.

'Are you Alison?' she asked, and it was an effort to speak.

A wary look came into the girl's eyes. 'Yes,' she said. 'Who are you?' She looked at her son, as though ready to snatch him up.

'My name's Jan Hunter,' Jan lied. 'Can I—talk to you?' She didn't want to talk. She wanted to hurt her, because whatever had gone on in the past was obviously still going on, and that was more horrible than anything else. It was like a nightmare.

'No,' said the girl. 'Are you a reporter?'

A reporter! A sob rose in Jan's throat. Had Sandor warned her? Had he already been in touch and told her not to say anything? 'No, I'm not,' she answered, fighting for calm. 'I'm a—I know Sandor.'

'I don't know you.' Alison came forward to the gate. 'Please go away. I don't want to talk to anyone—where is he? Did he send you?'

Close up, she was quite pretty, dark-haired, pale-skinned, with blue eyes, which held a defiant, almost frightened look. Jan felt a surge of pity for her. She no longer had the jealous urge to hurt. This girl was as much a victim as she was herself, for she too had fallen for the charm he undoubtedly possessed.

'It's all right,' she said. 'No, he didn't send me. He doesn't know I'm here.'

'Then how did you know where I lived?'

'I opened a letter to him by mistake.'

Alison's eyes widened. 'You had no right!'

'I know. It was a mistake—and I'm sorry. But I had to see for myself.'

'Well, now you have. Is that how you get your kicks? You in your posh car and clothes? I don't need to talk to you or anyone else. The only person I'll talk to is Sandor, so you can tell him that when you see him.' She turned away. 'Come on in, Nicky, it's time for your milk.' She scooped the child up, and turned back to face Jan. 'Go away! I'm going in now, and I don't want you following. I've made my life here—you're no part of it.' She began to walk away.

'Wait,' said Jan desperately. There was one question, only one more, but she must have the answer. On it depended her future life. 'Is it—is this child you're expecting also his?'

The girl turned, cheeks pink, eyes angry. 'What do *you* think?' she demanded. 'You want to mind your own business and let me mind mine!' Then she was gone, and the door slammed. Jan, shaken, stumbled back to her car. She sat in it for several minutes, incapable of movement. She had had her answer, and she wished she had never asked. She wished she had never left London, never met Sandor. It would have been better never to have loved at all than have this betrayal. How could he? How *could* he calmly keep a woman, have his child, and rarely see him?

Alison had begged him to see his son in the letter. When had his last visit been? Four or five months ago perhaps, enough time ago to have made her pregnant again. It was as if, suddenly, she saw him in a totally new light. She had thought him honest, but he had no conscience at all. He wanted what he wanted, and he got it. He had wanted Jan. The only odd thing was that he had bothered to marry her. He would not have needed to. . . .

She started the engine, her heart bitter, her eyes blind with tears. She didn't want to go back to the cottage where she had known such intense happiness that the thought of it now was agony. Yet she was finished with running away. And now there was nowhere to run. She would go back to Sandor and face him, tell him what she knew. And he would never touch her again.

She found a place to turn the car and drove back,

past the cottage where the girl stood at the window, and she didn't once look back.

Sandor came in the house for his lunch, and there was none ready. He walked into the kitchen, was about to say something, then, seeing Jan's face, paused.

'What is it?' he asked, after a moment. Jan looked at him. She was icily calm now, well under control.

'This is *it*,' she said, and handed him the letter, careful to keep her distance. 'I opened it by mistake—and then I went to see her.'

He read the letter, skimming over it, then looked up. His eyes had narrowed, his whole body had gone tense. 'I see,' he said slowly. 'I'm sorry you found out in this way. I was going to tell——'

'Please,' she breathed. 'Please spare me the platitudes. You were going to tell me? Of course you were —now I've found out! It's a bit too late, though, isn't it? How many more mistresses do you have on the go? Do you get them all pregnant?' Her voice rose. 'I mean, do you have a rota?'

'You're getting hysterical,' he said, and his voice, in contrast to hers, was dangerously quiet. 'And you have clearly misunderstood——'

'I've misunderstood nothing!' she shouted. 'There's not much to mistake when you see a girl who's obviously pregnant carrying your son under her arm. I mean, how much more stupid do I have to be?'

Sandor turned away and went over to the sink as if he didn't intend to answer, and she followed him and wrenched his arm, pulling him round. 'Answer me,' she demanded, her whole body trembling. 'Answer me or I'll hit you!'

'I'll answer you when you've calmed down,' he said evenly. His accent was more pronounced, a sure sign of temper smouldering, and his eyes had gone dark. 'Because you certainly would not listen to anything I have to say now——'

'You're damned right I wouldn't! Because it would all be a pack of lies. You've been seeing her all the time, haven't you? Using her—were you keeping her to one side to be used when you came to live down here? I mean, the women in London had grown stale, I imagine, and Alison's only *young*——'

'You are going too far.' He gripped her arms suddenly, violently. 'You are saying things you will regret later.'

'I won't regret this!' she spat out. 'You can sleep alone tonight—I don't want you to touch me!'

'Be sure of what you are saying,' he cut in. 'Be very sure——'

'I'm sure, all right. I thought I loved you——' Her voice broke with a sob.

'Where there is no trust, there can be no love,' he said quietly. 'If that is the way you feel, so be it. Excuse me, I have some food to prepare.' He released her and turned away from her. His movement had a sense of finality about it.

Jan watched him, a numbness spreading through her limbs, chilling her to the bone. Then she turned and walked out, up to their bedroom, and began to move her clothes out. It seemed as if her marriage of two days was over. It seemed as if life stretched ahead, grim, grey—and empty. But she wasn't going to run away. Somehow, she would survive.

Two days passed, and each moment of each hour of those two days was agony for Jan. Sandor scarcely spoke, and he was punctilious about not touching her, as if he could not bear to. She caught a glimpse of his face once, when he was not aware of her gaze, and saw a deep, secret pain, and almost reached out to touch him—but didn't. Her own misery was no less deep. She spent hours taking the dogs for long walks, and keeping the cottage immaculate, but it was not enough to fill the empty hours.

On the evening of the third day Sandor went out in his car. His words before he went were: 'I am going out.' That was all. Jan sat and watched a succession of programmes on the television without being aware of their content, the dogs nestling at her sides, and after three hours, when she could bear no more, she half filled a glass with whisky and drank it. It numbed her raw nerve ends, made the room hazy, and, without making her feel better, took away some of the pain, as an anaesthetic would.

She had gone out to the kitchen, walking very carefully, to make herself a cup of coffee, when she heard the front door open, and stiffened. It slammed shut, then Sandor was in the kitchen with her.

'I'm making myself coffee,' she said, slowly, carefully. 'Do you want some?'

'No.' He came over to where she stood beside the cooker, switched off the gas, and turned her round to face him. 'I am going to make love to you, I have waited long enough.'

'You're mad! You——'

'I am your husband,' he grated. 'Or had you forgotten?'

'How could I forget? I'm the only one you married, aren't I? More fool me.' She glared at him. 'Or perhaps I'm not. Are there any weddings you conveniently "forgot" to tell me about——' She got no further. Sandor grabbed hold of her and forced her head back with the pressure of his mouth. He wasn't drunk, but he had had a drink. He was also very, very strong.

Jan struggled vainly to free herself of the relentless hold, but it was useless. She felt her head swimming as he kissed her with a deep dark passion and savagery she had never known, and as his hands touched her body, not gently, but roughly, her mind was blindingly aware that there was no escape, that he meant what he said. He was going to make love to her and there was nothing she could do to stop him. Only it wouldn't be lovemaking, it would be rape.

Her struggles, as she tried to prevent him taking her sweater off, only served to quicken his own savage excitement, and she felt the sweater rip completely down the front, and tried to clutch it to her, moaning softly, dazed, her brain befuddled with the drink, aware, treacherously, and too late, of her own growing reponse to his excitement.

Then he was carrying her up the stairs, into the bedroom, where he flung her on the bed and watched her. Slowly he began to take off his clothes, and she looked at him, wanting him, hating him—hating herself——

'Now,' he said thickly. 'Now I will show you——' and his body was pressed on hers, and with his hands he began to strip her, relentless hands, no stopping them, or him, and now she did not want to.

His hands were fire and strength, his mouth burned hers, and his body knew what he wanted, and responded, as did Jan, then it was an aching ecstasy and torment, savagery and passion such as she had never dreamed existed, and the violent lovemaking mingled with her complete and utter surrender, until at last they cried out, then were still.

Sandor moved away from her, looking down where she lay helpless on the bed. 'Now you know how I shall take you any time I want you,' he said. 'And I will not ask.' He began to put on his clothes, and she watched him, her heart still fast beating with the punishment she had known, unable to move, to reply. He buckled his belt.

'Now, I will have my coffee,' he said. 'And tonight you will sleep in this bed with me. And if I want you again, I will have you. Do you understand?' Jan didn't reply. 'Do you understand?' he repeated.

'Yes,' she whispered.

He walked out without another word and, shakily,

Jan got to her feet. She had just learned something about herself, but as yet she wasn't prepared to think about it.

CHAPTER EIGHT

JAN knew what it was she had learned about herself during the night when, lying awake beside her sleeping husband, she realised that the love she felt for him was as deep as ever. Regardless of what he had done, or been, or was, her heart knew what her mind had tried to deny. She loved him instinctively, blindly, all her senses aware of him in every way. She loved the way he looked, and moved, and spoke; she loved everything about him. Little wonder that other women had felt as she did. Little wonder that he had managed to bowl her mother over. She moved restlessly, agonised at the misery of the gulf between them which had turned him into a hard-eyed stranger, who took without giving, who looked at her with eyes that were blank of all save physical desire for her—and he woke with her movement, and drowsily, still more asleep than awake, let his arm fall across her. Her heart began to beat faster and she let herself go nearer to him, knowing, sensing, what would happen, and wanting him as she had never wanted any man before.

His half sleeping hand came to life, and he moved it nearer her heart, then his breathing changed and she sensed he was coming awake. Sandor groaned something and began to caress her, still as though asleep, but she knew he wasn't. There was now the sensation of being in a dream, each movement with its purpose, but slow and unhurried, and it was as though there were all the time in the world for what must inevitably happen. It was a slow-motion dream, and his lips were against her cheek now, his breath a gentle movement like all his others, and she felt the warmth of his body, the growing awareness of her that he was experiencing; her limbs were cool and inviting against him, and then he was nearer, much too near for safety, and yet she had never felt so safe in her life as she did now. His hands were moving with an expertise that filled her with wonder and she wanted to cry out, to tell him, but was silent. His breath quickened as his lips came down on hers, and she knew she was lost, as surely as he was, she knew that he wanted her more than he had ever wanted any other woman, and she moved to let him see. Then it was timeless, exquisite, so wonderful, too beautiful for words, or for anything else. . . .

In the morning she awoke, and he had gone. She could hear movement from downstairs, the rattle of crockery, the kettle beginning to boil, and she waited there, lying back, savouring the memory of Sandor's lovemaking, reliving it in her mind until she was warm with the memories, and aching for him. Then the door slammed, and there was silence. He had gone out. Jan heard his car start up, and went to the window to see him driving away. Then she remembered that she had heard the telephone ringing, and she had thought it was in her sleep then, but now she knew it was real.

She was wide awake. Something was happening, and she didn't know what it was, but she was uneasy. She

pulled on a dressing gown to hide her nakedness and
went downstairs. She had her second shock when she
saw the time. It was not yet seven. A half empty cup of
tea stood on the table, and the dogs were waiting to go
out. Her heart started to beat faster. Where had Sandor
gone? There was no note, nothing. She opened the
door and let Domino and Finn into the garden, then
switched on the gas under the still warm kettle. She began to shiver because she was frightened, and she
didn't know why, which made it worse. A picture of
Alison standing at the door of her house came into her
head—suddenly she knew where he had gone, and she
closed her eyes. Dear God, no, she thought. Not now,
not after—but he could, and if it was a punishment, it
was the worst he could have devised. It was worse than
anything.

If he was there. If—there was one way to check. She
could phone the number she had memorised, and ask
for him. Then she would know for sure. But now she
wasn't sure if she wanted to know at all. She made herself a cup of tea and looked at the telephone standing
silently in the hall. She had only to pick it up and dial,
in, say, ten minutes—and she would know. And what
then? What do I do then? she thought. Run away
again? Or stay and fight, because I love him? The only
trouble was, how could she fight a woman who had
already borne him one child and was carrying the
second?

They had discussed children before the wedding,
and Sandor wanted two or three, he had told her. Jan
remembered now she had laughed at that, and agreed

that yes, three was an ideal number, or maybe four, two of each—and she wanted so much to bear his child because she had sensed he would be a good, loving father. Only he wasn't. He was a casual father, seeing his són only rarely, paying, probably well, for his upkeep, but not caring about the responsibility....

She wept for Nicky then, for the little boy she had seen so briefly who was the image of Sandor, and who probably loved him. And she wept for Alison who probably still loved him, and hoped, and had been deceived—and lastly, she wept for herself.

She let the dogs in, and it was time. It was now or never. Wait, and she would lack the courage, and perhaps never really know. She picked up the telephone and dialled, and she was going to ask to speak to him, then hang up. But she didn't need to ask, for it was Sandor who answered. She put the telephone down, and looked at it, white with shock. Now, now she really knew.

The next two hours were such agony that they were almost unbearable. Her vivid imagination supplied the pictures she didn't need, or want, but they refused to go away. She saw Sandor playing in the garden with his son, while Alison looked on, she saw him going into the house and kissing Alison, telling her he loved her and would always look after her, she saw the little boy reaching up to be held in his father's arms, and almost heard Sandor laughing as he picked his son up....

'Stop it!' she cried, and the dogs looked at her in

puzzlement, sensing her distress, wanting to help, but only able to lick her hand as she stood in the lounge by the window, her eyes dry now because there were no more tears to shed, only a pain in her that would not go away. What was he telling Alison? That his marriage was a mistake? That he had met and married in haste? That——

She heard his car before she saw it, and waited there calmly for it to draw up. She was too exhausted to be otherwise. Nothing could hurt her more, now. Whatever Sandor did or said, she had already been through all the possibilities in her mind, and there was nothing more to surprise her.

Except what she saw as he got out of the car, leaned in the back, and lifted out his son. She went icily cold all over. That, she had not imagined. Not that. She stood and watched him carrying the little boy towards the house, and numbly went to open the door as they came up the path. Nicky was in pyjamas, and was rubbing his eyes sleepily.

'I'm going to put Nicky up in bed for a while,' Sandor said, and looked at her. 'Make me some toast, will you?' He grinned at the little boy. 'A little sleep for you, then you can come down and meet our nice dogs.' He ran up the stairs lightly, and Jan saw the little puzzled, tired face looking down at her over Sandor's shoulder before they vanished. She walked out to the kitchen in a daze and put bread in the toaster.

She heard Sandor come in behind her, but she didn't turn. 'Was it you who rang?' he demanded.

'Yes.'

'I thought so. Alison has gone into hospital with a threatened miscarriage——' She turned then, dismay mingled with the shock.

'Oh—I'm sorry,' she gasped.

'Are you?' His eyes were cold. 'I'm taking care of Nicky. She has no one else near to do so. A neighbour phoned me to tell me.'

'I see.' She had to swallow. Her throat had gone very dry. 'I'll look after him, of course. You have your work——'

'He's my responsibility.' He didn't say 'he's my son', but the words didn't need to be said.

'I know,' she said quietly, 'but he needs a woman to look after him. Don't worry, I'll care for him as though——' she faltered, 'he were my own son.'

'Thank you.' He looked at her, and some of the coldness had gone.

Jan took the toast and buttered it, and handed it to him. 'His clothes are in the car,' he said. 'I took what I could find. Anything else he needs, I'll buy.'

'I'll go and get them in.' All her fevered imaginings hadn't covered this. Sandor didn't seem like a man in torment over the woman he loved being ill, but perhaps he wasn't. He didn't seem anything, except like a stranger again, not the same man who had taken her twice to the very brink of ecstasy and back so recently. He merely looked tired, which was hardly surprising. She left him eating and went out to his car. Two plastic shopping bags lay on the back seat, together with a blanket and the pillow the boy had clearly slept on on his journey. Jan took everything into the house, left it in the hall, and went out in the kitchen to see Sandor preparing to leave.

'I shall be working on the house,' he said. 'Call me if you need me.' For my son, he meant, not if *you* need me.

'Of course. But I'll manage. Are you—will you be going to see Alison in hospital?'

'Yes, this evening. I won't take Nicky, it might upset him.'

'Of course. I'll have your lunch ready at one. Will that be all right?'

'Perfectly.' He looked at her, then went out.

Jan crept up the stairs and looked in the spare bedroom to see the little boy fast asleep, thumb in mouth, clutching the teddy he had brought with him. She smiled, then crept downstairs again. Now, strangely enough, she felt better. She had someone else to think about instead of herself and her own problems. She had no idea what kind of food a four-year-old ate, but she was going to find out. She picked up the telephone and dialled an old friend in London, Christina, who was the mother of lively four-year-old twins. She would know, better than anyone.

It was a pleasant surprise, and quite a relief, to discover that a four-year-old can eat practically anything an adult can, within reason, and that feeding Nicky was going to be no problem.

At eleven Jan went up to find him awake, and rather tearful. She knew she had to handle him carefully for the first few minutes, and on this would depend his happiness while he was there. 'Hello, Nicky,' she said warmly. 'I'm Jan. It's nice to see you're awake. Would you like to come down for a drink of milk, and meet two nice dogs? They're looking forward to seeing you.'

He frowned. 'Sando said he had two doggies, but I'm not sure if I like them.'

So he called his father 'Sando'. She would have to get used to that.

'Well, we'll go and see, shall we?' she said brightly, praying inwardly that he would. It would be difficult to keep the huge dogs shut out of his way all the time if he was frightened, which he might well be, for they would undoubtedly tower over him. She crossed her fingers quickly, superstitiously, and lifted back the covers. 'Then when you've had your milk, you can get dressed. Do you dress yourself?'

' 'Course. I'm nearly *four*,' he said with scorn.

She hid a grin. 'That's *super*. I thought you were six. You're a big boy, aren't you?'

He grinned back at her impishly, and her heart lifted in relief. He liked her. He might not like the dogs, but he liked her. It was one hurdle overcome. She held out her hand and Nicky slid out of bed and took hold of hers. Then they went down the stairs very slowly, Jan talking all the while. 'There they are. That's Domino, and that one's Finn. Look, they're wagging their tails. They *are* pleased to see you. We'll be able to take them long walks and go paddling. Do you like paddling, Nicky? Here, Domino, come and say hello to Nicky. He's four—nearly.'

The large gentle dog, ever willing to please, and intelligent enough to sense what was in Jan's voice, ambled over and wagged his long tail and allowed Nicky to touch his head. Then it was Finn's turn, and he did the same. Jan praised them profusely, telling them they were very good dogs, and they all went into the kitchen for milk. Hurdle number two safely over.

Nicky sat at the table holding the beaker in his chubby hands and looked at Jan. 'I want my mummy,' he said.

Jan's heart sank. 'She's gone away just for a day or two, so Sando said he'd like to have you here with us. Then you'll go home to Mummy. It'll be *fun* here, you know. You can draw and paint and I'll get you some toys——'

'Why did she go away?' His mouth quivered, and Finn walked over and rested his head on the little boy's knee and looked sadly at him, tail going slowly. It gave Jan an idea.

'Oh, look,' she said, 'look at Finn. He doesn't want you to cry. He wants to look after you! Tell you what, give him that biscuit I put out for you and I'll get two more, and you can give Domino one as well. Then you can tell your mummy how they liked you.'

It had the effect—temporarily at least—of distracting him from his tearful question. He handed the huge dog a biscuit, and Finn took it from him, careful not to touch the boy's hands, only the biscuit, and Nicky chuckled.

'Look, Jan,' he exclaimed. 'He likes biscuits.' He pronounced it bikkits.

'He does indeed.' Jan sat down, letting her breath out in a little silent 'phew' of relief. Domino's turn next, and he too took the proffered 'bikkit' with great good manners.

After that the ice was broken, and Nicky sat at the kitchen table and watched Jan peel potatoes and carrots to go with the steak pie for lunch. He insisted on helping, so she gave him a second, rather blunt potato peeler and a potato and demonstrated its use.

By the time lunch was ready he was dressed in jeans and tee-shirt, washed and hair brushed, clutching his teddy bear, and hungry. Sandor walked in to see the little boy sitting at the table drawing a picture on a large sheet of paper with one of Sandor's fibre-tipped pens. He lifted an eyebrow and gave a half smile at Jan, who said:

'Nicky's been helping me with the lunch.'

'Has he now? That is good. I see you have found some paper and a pen. I shall have to find you some more. Come with me, Nicky.' He held out his hand and the little boy slid off the chair and took Sandor's hand.

'Have you any crayons?' he asked, looking up bright-eyed.

Sandor grinned. 'We shall have to see, won't we?

Come.' They went out. Jan watched them go. Oh, what a mess it all was, a stupid, tragic mess. Sandor and his son looked so right together, somehow. He should be with him all the time, and with Alison, who had loved him enough—and almost certainly still did—to bear his children. Perhaps that was why he had moved here— only I've spoiled it, she thought. I never wanted to spoil anyone's life like that. I should never have come. If I hadn't this illness of Alison's might have served to bring them together. . . .

Her thoughts were interrupted by the return of Sandor and Nicky, carrying a pile of paper, Nicky clutching a handful of vari-coloured fibre-tipped pens. But a seed had been sown in her mind. . . .

'Lunch is nearly ready,' she said briskly. 'We'll eat first, I think, then Nicky and I will have a busy after-noon drawing.' She smiled at them both, even though her heart was torn.

'That sounds very nice.' Sandor lifted his son up on to a chair and put the drawing materials to one side. Jan served the meal, having first chopped Nicky's portion into bite-sized pieces, and all went well. The boy ate everything that was put in front of him, and had choco-late biscuits and milk afterwards, and the dogs sat silently by him, in case any crumbs should fall, and she knew then that she was going to manage. She won-dered how long he would stay. In a strange way it was as though he were her own child. Hers and Sandor's. She wondered how much Sandor loved him, if he was glad that Nicky was there. His face gave no indication.

He was gentler, gentler with them both when Nicky was there, and it made her heart ache, and she sensed that there would be changes over the next few days. It seemed to her that she loved him so much that she would let him go, if that was what he wanted.

Jan knew she had led a fairly selfish, unthinking life. Wealth had cushioned her existence from any harsh realities. But she sensed that she too would change. And all because of one small boy.

Leaving Nicky drawing at the table, she followed Sandor out of the back door when he left to go to work. 'May I have a word with you?' She felt as if she were talking to a stranger.

He paused, turned. 'Of course. What is it?'

'It's about Nicky. He was asking where his mother was. Am I to tell him if he asks again?'

He frowned. 'Say she is having a rest in a nice place for a day or so, but will soon be home again. Tell him to do a picture for her and that I will take it tonight.'

'Yes, I will.' She looked into his eyes. 'He's very well behaved. I don't think he'll be any trouble. He's a nice boy.'

'He is.' He smiled. 'Is that all? I must go.'

'Of course.' Jan flushed, feeling as if she had been reprimanded. His eyes, too, were those of a stranger. She turned away before he could see the hurt in her own eyes, went in, and closed the door. 'Now, Nicky,' she said, 'Sando wants you to do a drawing for your mummy, and he'll give it to her.'

His face brightened. 'Yes. What shall I do?'

'Why don't you draw the dogs? She'd like to see those.'

He clapped his hands. 'Yes, I will. Is she coming home soon?'

'Very soon. She's having a rest in a nice place, because she's a bit tired.'

He sighed. 'Will you look after me?'

'Of course I will!' She went over impulsively, picked him up, and hugged him. His chubby hands went round her neck and he kissed her cheek, then giggled.

'That's nice,' she said. 'Thank you.' But she didn't want him to see the tears that sprang into her eyes. She put him down on the chair and pulled up another near him, then sat down herself.

'Now, I think I'll draw *you* while you're drawing the dogs. That'll be funny, won't it?' She blinked a few times, and all was well.

'Mmm, funny.' Nicky bent over the paper and began to draw laboriously, with much sighing and sticking of tongue at corner of mouth, and for a while they worked in silence. Jan watched him, not sure whether she wanted to laugh or cry at the concentration which was resulting in the most amazing circles and squiggles, all brightly coloured.

She made coffee for herself after a while, gave him a beaker of milk, and then, sensing he would soon be bored, suggested taking the dogs out for a walk. He seemed to think this was a good idea and went to fetch his jacket while Jan tidied the table. Then they set off to walk along the sands.

Nicky was asleep in bed at six-thirty when Sandor came in from work, dirty and exhausted. 'I'm going to have a bath,' he said, surveying his plaster-whitened hands. 'Then I will go to the hospital.'

'Nicky's had his tea. He's asleep now—please don't wake him. Shall I run your water?'

'No, thank you. And I will eat when I return.'

Jan pointed to a milk bottle full of wild flowers. 'Nicky picked those for—for Alison. I'll put them in paper and roll up his picture ready for you to take.'

Sandor looked at the crammed bottle and gave a little smile. 'Very nice,' he commented. 'Whose idea was that?'

'Nicky's,' Jan lied. She didn't want him to know, for reasons she didn't understand, that she had thought of the flowers. Perhaps, she thought, in some faint surprise when Sandor had gone up for his bath, I'm beginning to think of other people. . . .

The minute he had gone she filled the washer with dirty clothes, and set up the ironing board to iron some shirts for Sandor. She could not settle to sit and watch television, and work was the only answer for the restless unhappiness that filled her.

She was tired when he returned, but his chicken salad was ready waiting, and she put it on the table when he came in. 'I'll have to go to the village to-morrow,' she said. 'Nicky needs some vests and pants and I'd like to stock up with more tinned food.'

'Do you want me to take you?'

'No, I'll take Nicky with me. I'll manage. How was Alison?'

'She'll be in for a day or so while they do tests. They're not sure if she's lost the baby yet.' He looked up at her. 'She's very relieved that Nicky is being well looked after. She cried when I gave her the flowers and picture.'

Jan smiled. It hurt, but she smiled. It would have been much easier to weep. She didn't know what was happening to her.

'I'm going to have a bath and an early night,' she said, and waited for his reply.

He scarcely looked up from his salad. 'Fine. I have some work to do and I may be late. But I will take the dogs out before I go to bed.'

She was effectively dismissed. Very quietly she gathered up the ironed shirts and walked out of the kitchen.

She read in bed, because she knew she wouldn't sleep, and at ten-thirty went to check that Nicky was all right. From downstairs a light shone from the lounge, and she heard faint music from the record player. She stood for a moment on the landing looking down, an empty sadness within her. So quickly had everything changed. How brief had been the happiness. She closed her eyes, but there were no tears to shed; the ache was a dry one, and it was more painful than anything that had gone before. Silently she turned and went back into the bedroom, and switched off the light.

The moon filled the room with a cool, eerie light, and she gazed wide-eyed at the window. She could hear the sea, faintly, soothing, reassuring, constant. It was so beautiful there, so achingly beautiful. How perfect it could have been. . . .

She heard sounds, Sandor calling the dogs, then a door closing, and she knew he would be coming up to bed. Turning on her side, she pulled the covers up and closed her eyes, and waited.

He went into Nicky's room after the bathroom, and Jan heard a soft murmur, then he was in the bedroom with her, and she heard the rustle of his clothes, the clunk of his belt hitting the chair, then his weight on the bed. Eyes closed, heart beating erratically, she lay there feigning sleep. She needn't have bothered. Within minutes she heard his deep steady breathing and knew he was asleep. She lay awake for a while longer before falling asleep herself.

She woke once during the night because she heard words, broken, muttered, anguished-sounding words, not in English. Save one, repeated, and it sounded like 'Alison'. She fell into a troubled sleep after that, a restless, nightmare-filled sleep. Yet the memory of the words was gone by morning. It was much later in the day before she recalled them. . . .

She enjoyed the morning's shopping with Nicky. He was good company, full of wonder at the shops—and she bought him several toys so that the car was loaded up by the time they were ready for home again. It was nearly lunchtime. Nicky sat in the back clutching the wooden walking dog she had bought for him, and talked non-stop. She listened only vaguely at first, nodding and agreeing, concentrating on her driving, until he said, 'I like you, Jan.'

'Do you? Thank you, that's nice. I like you too.'

'An' I like the dogs—I'm going to show them my doggy, they'll like *that*—an' I like Sando 'cos he's very kind to me an' my mummy——' It was like a sudden pain, a shock.

'Of course he is,' Jan agreed, voice deceptively calm. 'He's a very kind man.'

'Do you like Sando?'

'Of course I do—and the dogs.' Please change the subject, she prayed, but her mind was blank. She couldn't for anything have thought of something different to talk about.

'When he comes to see us he brings me presents. Do you like presents?'

'Oh yes, I do,' she agreed. 'This car was a present from my mummy.'

'An' he brings my mummy presents too. He gave her a lovely tele—tele——' he stopped, frowning.

'Television?'

'Mmm, yes. I watch Play-school. I *like* that.'

'I'm sure you do. We must watch it today, mustn't we?'

'Mmm, yes, I'd like that. But my uncle—the other one, you know—he buys us presents as well.'

His words fell into a stunned silence. What other

man? How could she ask? 'That's nice,' she said weakly. Oh God, it was getting worse—unless the uncle was perhaps Alison's brother.

'Uncle who?' she asked gently.

'Brian—you know—but he goes away *a lot*.'

'Ah, I see.' But she didn't. She felt totally confused. Did Sandor know about 'Uncle Brian'? She had to ask. She had to know.

'Is he your mummy's brother?'

'Mmm, yes, I think so. He's nice.'

'Yes, I'm sure he is.' A faint hope, so faint as to be almost invisible, vanished. Jan concentrated on her driving. What had she hoped? She didn't want to think about it. 'We'll soon be home,' she said. 'And this afternoon we'll have lots to do, won't we?'

Nicky began to jump up and down in the back, nearly rocking the car. 'Wait till the doggies see my toys!' he exclaimed. 'Won't they be s'prised?' He chuckled. 'I like staying with you and Sando. I hope my mummy can come and stay too.'

'Yes, so do I.' But she didn't. She didn't really want to see Alison again if she could help it. It would hurt too much. It was just as well she didn't know about the telephone message that awaited her on her return. And she hadn't yet recalled the words she had heard during the night.

CHAPTER NINE

SANDOR was waiting for them as they walked up the path. He came forward to take the crammed shopping bags from Jan, and expressed delight at the dog Nicky was proudly brandishing. There was something that disturbed Jan in his eyes as he looked at her.

He led the way into the kitchen and they followed. 'Nicky,' he said, 'why don't you go and put all these lovely toys in the lounge and I will come and see them in a minute? I wish to talk to Jan for a moment.'

Nicky began to gather the toys together in his arms and tottered out, loaded up. Jan looked at Sandor.

'What is it?' she asked quietly.

His eyes were very serious. 'I telephoned the hospital because, last evening, they asked me to. Alison will be discharged tomorrow.'

'Oh, I see.' She knew there was more to come. She did not, at that moment, guess what it was.

'She is not well enough to look after herself.' He paused. 'She has not lost the baby, but she well might if she doesn't have complete rest. The hospital has had an outbreak of infection in the maternity ward and it is essential that only the most necessary cases stay——'

Jan knew what she had to say. It didn't make it any easier, but she knew she had to do it. 'She must come here,' she said. 'There's room. I might not be a nurse, but I can see that she gets all the rest she needs.' She knew that her face was white, because she had felt the blood drain from it as he spoke. She knew that it had to happen, and in a way it might decide things, once and for all. She could not go on the rest of her life never being sure, not knowing.

'Are you sure?'

'Yes, I'm sure. There's no choice, is there?'

'I could employ a nurse to look after her in her own house——'

'That won't be necessary.' Her head felt very light, as if she might float away at any moment, but she faced him, chin lifted, her head held proudly. 'I'll look after her and Nicky here. He's settled now, he likes it here—and besides——' for a moment her voice faltered, 'they need you.' She turned and walked steadily into the lounge.

It was much later, after tea, when she was bathing Nicky before bed, that she remembered waking up and hearing Sandor's words in the night, and she held on to the side of the bath, because for a moment, the room had swum round. He had cried out for Alison in his sleep. Had he also been thinking of her those times that he had made love to her? The idea was unbearable.

'Look, Jan, look!' A violent splash as Nicky's new plastic duck hit the water drenched her—it also wrenched her back to the present.

She stood up. 'Oh! Look at my blouse!'

His eyes filled, and his mouth trembled, and she added hastily: 'I'm not cross, love.' She knelt down again and caught hold of the duck. 'I'm going to splash *you* for that, young Master Duck.' And she did so. The near-tears changed to laughter as Nicky joined in— and it was at that moment that Sandor walked in. He stood for a few seconds watching them, and Nicky shouted:

'Look at this naughty duck, he splashed Jan!' Eyes shining, he looked at Sandor, who smiled.

'I shall not come too near then,' he said. 'I don't want that to happen to me.' He looked at Jan. 'I must leave now. I shall call at the house on my way there for her clothes. I shall be gone about two hours.'

'Very well. I'll get everything ready tonight,' she said quietly. She turned to the little boy. 'Out you come! You're lovely and clean—and I think I'll read you a story to get you to sleep. Would you like that?' She was learning the dismissing game as well. She lifted him out and wrapped the large red fluffy towel around him. 'There we go.' She heard Sandor walking out, but she didn't look round. A minute later she heard the front door closing, followed by his car starting up.

When he returned from the hospital she was watching television, and when he came into the lounge she looked up and said: 'We could do with a small camp bed for Nicky to sleep in. Aunt Jessie has one in the spare bedroom. Could you get it out, please?'

'Yes, of course.'

'Is she coming here by ambulance?'

'No, I am going to fetch her at nine in my car.'

'I see.' Jan stood up. 'When you've got the bed I'll make it up. I've washed all the necessary sheets. Then

I shall write some letters in the bedroom if you're working down here.'

For a moment they faced each other, then he spoke quietly. 'We have a lot of things to talk about, Jan— we both know it, and I must——'

'No,' she said breathlessly. 'No. Don't you *see*? I don't want to hear!'

'But you must listen. I have waited, I have been patient, waiting for you to come to your senses——'

'My senses? I came to my senses the day I opened a letter by mistake!'

'Things are not always what they seem,' he said, his temper rising to match hers.

'They're probably worse,' said Jan, her voice low and vibrant; she was shaking.

He caught hold of her arms. 'You will listen——'

'Let me be!' She wrenched herself free and hit him hard across his face, backing away as though he would strike her in return. 'I hate you—I despise you!' she hissed. 'But I'll look after your mistress and your child —because perhaps it's a lesson I have to learn—per- haps it's a punishment. But don't touch me ever again!' and she whirled away from him and went out. She saw his face before she went, and the memory of it was to haunt her for a long time. He had gone white, and he looked as though something in him had died. And he looked angry enough to kill her.

She thought it would be agony for her to see Alison arriving at the house. But it wasn't. As Jan stood at the

door with Nicky, watching Sandor carry her up the
path towards them, her heart reached out in a strange
kind of pain and empathy. She too had suffered. And
she looked so young, so vulnerable, her face drained of
all colour, her eyes on Jan's in a kind of piteous appeal,
as if she feared her dislike.

Jan smiled, though her heart ached. 'Welcome,
Alison,' she said quietly. 'Nicky's been waiting for you
since breakfast.' She lifted the little boy up and he
kissed his mother's cheek and burst into tears.

Five minutes later Alison was in bed, Nicky cuddled
up to her, and Jan sat on the edge of the bed. 'I've
made up a camp bed for Nicky,' she said, 'in the corner.
But he can stay in——' she was going to say 'our
room', but the words wouldn't come out. 'In another
bedroom if you prefer.'

Alison smiled faintly. 'I'd rather have him here with
me,' she said, and kissed him.

'Then he shall be. Sandor's gone to make you a cup
of tea. He won't be a minute.' Jan had not spoken to
him since a terrible scene the previous night, before
she had slept on the settee downstairs. She would not
do so again. He had made it quite clear what would
happen if she did, and she didn't intend a repeat of the
scene that followed.

He had come down, followed her downstairs when
he had seen her taking blankets and pillows, and gone
into the lounge after her, closing the door, shutting the
dogs out.

'What are you doing?' he had demanded.

'I should think it's obvious,' she retorted, and dumped the blankets on the settee.

'Not to me. Explain.' He had waited, he was going to have an answer, one way or another.

'I don't want to sleep with you.'

'You are my wife.'

'Am I? I still don't want to sleep with you.' She had turned away then, in dismissal. But this time Sandor was not to be dismissed.

He stepped forward, caught hold of her, and swung her round. 'Then don't,' he snapped. 'I will sleep alone. But first——' and he began to undo her dressing gown. Jan had fought and struggled, but in vain. The struggles only excited him further, and he was like a man possessed as he held her, writhing, in his arms. Then suddenly they were on the settee, in a tangle of blankets and pillows, and the excitement grew in her, even though she thought she hated him, and became a fever that swept them along on a frenzied tide of mutual physical desire that could have only one, inevitable, ending.

When at last, spent and exhausted, she lay trembling in the aftermath of a savage lovemaking, Sandor stood up and looked down at her, and smiled. 'Just remember,' he said huskily, 'I shall take you whenever and wherever I want.' Then he had gathered up his clothes and walked out, leaving her completely shattered. She had pulled up a blanket to cover her nakedness, curled up on the settee, and gone straight to sleep in sheer exhaustion.

Now, looking at Alison, she wondered if he had ever treated her like that. Somehow she doubted it. Her face had a freshness about it, almost an innocence, and trust. She was only young—she hardly seemed old enough to be the mother of a four-year-old boy, but she was. 'I'll be glad of a drink,' she said. 'I hope Nicky's not being any trouble.'

'He's very good,' smiled Jan. 'And he says he's going to do lots of pictures for you. That'll be nice, won't it?'

'Lovely. I—er—didn't know you were married to Sandor, Jan. I'm sorry if I was abrupt with you, but he'd warned me not to talk——' Alison stopped, and flushed, her eyes miserable.

'Please, don't apologise,' Jan said hastily. She didn't want to discuss anything. To do so would be agony for her, but on the other hand she had to clear the air before Sandor came up again. 'Let's forget about it, shall we? You're going to stay here until you're better, that's the only important thing.' She smiled at the girl in the bed, but her heart ached. Sandor must love Alison. She had a certain beauty about her, a shyness that would be appealing, and a round young face and blue eyes. Jan was beginning to know what she would have to do soon —but not yet. She needed more courage before she took the step she had to take.

She stood up. 'He's here now. I'm going to prepare lunch. I hope you've got as good an appetite as your son.' She opened the door for Sandor, waited until he was in, said: 'I'll leave you to talk while I go and prepare the food,' and went out.

In the kitchen alone, she thought over Alison's words. Alison had apologised to Jan because, she said, she had not known they were married. Did she accept it then, just like that? Did she love Sandor enough not to mind that he had married another woman? Jan's head began to ache with the sheer pressure of her own confusions and doubts. Insistently returning was the awful, guilt-inducing thought that she herself had been responsible for Alison's threatened miscarriage. That was almost unbearable, and even before, when she had first insisted on Alison's coming to the cottage to be looked after, it must already have been in her subconscious mind.

There was only one course of action now, if she were to assuage her guilt. Alison would be well cared for, as would Nicky. They would want for nothing. When Sandor came down, carrying his son, she was composed and ready for him.

'Please tell me,' she said, 'exactly what they told you at the hospital about Alison's care. Is she to be allowed up or not? Is there any medicine she needs?'

He put the boy down. 'She has to have bed rest for a couple of days. The local doctor—the one you saw— has been contacted, and will call later today. I suggest you talk to him. As for medicine, they said nothing, merely that it was essential she had her daily iron and vitamins. I have them in the car with her clothes.'

'Will you fetch them? I'll see she takes them. I'll see the doctor when he's looked at her. You might as well go to work now, everything is under control.' She looked coolly, calmly at him.

'Are you sure?'

'Quite sure.' She lifted Nicky on to a chair. 'You can help me get Mummy's dinner ready.' She looked up suddenly, too suddenly, to surprise a look she found disturbing on Sandor's face. Then it was gone. But the memory of it lingered for a while afterwards.

The days passed, and a routine was established that worked very well. Alison grew gradually better and stronger, and Jan felt a quiet satisfaction in seeing the colour return to the other's cheeks. One morning, at the weekend, she thought it would be all right, as Alison had asked, to let her and Nicky go for a walk along the sands. The two set out, and Jan watched them go, then dashed back to do some ironing.

Her days were filled from morning to night with work. It helped to blank out the misery. It was hard for her to feel sorry for herself when there was a mountain of washing to hang out, rooms to be vacuumed and dusted, and dishes to wash. She had established a routine, part of which was a quiet ten minutes with feet up and a cup of coffee mid-morning.

She left the ironing and went to have this break now, and when it was over, and Alison and Nicky still hadn't returned, she walked out of the garden and over the grass to look for them. What she saw made her heart stop for a moment, then begin to thud.

The girl stood talking to Sandor on the beach, while

Nicky played nearby with some shells. Jan had been about to call. She stopped, and watched instead. Sandor put his hand on Alison's arm, and she looked up at him, and Jan could imagine the trust and love in her eyes. She felt excluded, cut off, a stranger apart from the little scene, and she turned away and stumbled back blindly across the grass to the cottage.

There was a hollow ache, an agony of loneliness inside her. Sandor and she had scarcely spoken, save in the other's company, for several days. And he had not once touched her. Now—now she knew why. She felt physically sick, and utterly wretched. Before, he might not have loved her, but there had been his desire for her. Now there was nothing. But then would even he be able to make love to Jan with Alison living in the same house? Apparently not. She was in the kitchen. In her sudden anguish she swept her arm out, and knocked to the floor two glasses which had been draining on the mat at the side of the sink.

'Oh God!' Nearly in tears, she bent to sweep up the pieces before the dogs, which were in the back garden, could come back in. She had nearly finished when she heard the front door opening, and in her haste picked up a large piece clumsily and sliced her finger open. She must have cried out, because she heard Sandor rush in, but it was too late. The room spun madly round, there was a rushing sound in her ears, and everything went mercifully blank.

When she came round her finger was bandaged, she was lying on the settee in the lounge, and she felt extremely light-headed. Sandor knelt by her side holding a damp cloth which he had just applied to her face, judging by the coldness she felt on her forehead.

'Do not try to speak,' he said. 'Alison is making you a drink.'

'The glass——' Jan began.

'Is cleared up. All is well.'

'I must—do—lunch——' She struggled to sit up and he pushed her gently down.

'No, I shall do that.'

'But I want——' frantically she tried to push away his restraining hand. She had to work, to keep on working. It was the only thing which would keep her going, keep her safe—and sane.

'No. For now you rest. I did not realise—you have been working very hard——'

'I can *manage*,' she whispered fiercely. 'I *have* to, don't you see?'

'Yes, of course you can.' What was it about him that was different? Had he and Alison managed to have a private talk? Had they come to a decision? His dark face, shadowed to Jan because the light was behind him, was inscrutable, lean and hard. He was now a stranger to her. The gulf which had begun days ago was so wide it would never be bridged.

Jan had rarely thought of Jeremy in the past weeks. Now she did. As she looked at her stranger husband, she wondered what she would be doing if she had never escaped from London. They would be on honeymoon. She shivered. She had escaped, she knew that now, from what would have been a loveless, sterile marriage, but to what? This was worse, far worse.

It's me, she thought, with a flash of sudden, terrible insight. I'm incapable of loving or being loved. Perhaps I always will be. And I can't blame my mother. Ultimately, it is me. She knew now what she had to do if she was not to ruin any more lives. The decision made, she relaxed slightly, and lay back. Sandor frowned.

'You will rest for a while?'

'Yes, I will.'

'Good.' He stood up. 'Stay there—ah, here is Alison. A strong cup of tea will do you good.' He took the cup from Alison and handed it to Jan. Then he went out. Alison sat on a stool by the settee.

'I'm sorry,' she said. 'I know there's a lot of work in running a house. You've been awfully good.' She spoke shyly, hesitantly. Jan wanted to hate her. It would have been easier—but she couldn't. They were both victims. 'I'm going to do more, while I'm here. Soon I'll be all right. I've imposed on you long enough.'

Jan wanted to cry. Alison seemed to mean it. But she didn't know that Jan had seen Sandor and her talking so quietly on the beach. That was not easily forgotten. I'm the outsider, she wanted to cry. I'm the one who has no right here. You belong. Instead she said: 'That's all right, we'll manage somehow.' She finished the hot sweet tea, which had done the trick. 'Sandor's getting lunch ready.' She looked at her bandaged finger ruefully. 'That was stupid of me, wasn't it?'

'You were tired. It's easy to make mistakes when you're tired. Why don't you go and lie down for an hour?'

But that would be a form of running away, of absconding from responsibility. Jan shook her head. 'No, I'm fine.' Nicky rushed in at that moment, flung himself on his mother and regarded Jan solemnly.

'Are you poorly?' he asked.

Jan laughed. 'No, I'm fine now. See?' She waggled her bandaged finger for him to see. 'But I won't be able to wash up for a while!'

'I'll do it,' he announced. 'Can I, Mummy?'

Alison laughed. 'We'll see. Stay and talk to Jan and I'll go and help Sando.' She put him beside Jan on the settee, grinned at her, and, picking up Jan's beaker, went out. The dogs squeezed in through the partly open door and sprawled at Jan's feet.

She heard their voices from the kitchen, Alison laughing at something Sandor said. 'Tell you what,' said Jan, ever so brightly, 'let's play I-Spy, shall we?'

'What's that?' He was alert and interested.

'Mmm—well, you're supposed to know how to spell, but we'll do the sounds. See—I say, I spy with my little eye, something beginning with D. Do you know D? It's a duh sound.'

'Duh, duh——' Nicky looked round him. 'Doggies?'

'Well done! That's it! Right, now your turn.'

'I spy wiv my little eye something beginning wiv— er—muh.'

'Muh? Hmm, mantelpiece?'

'No.' He was hugging himself gleefully.

'Magazine?'

'No!' he squealed. 'Shall I tell you?'

'Yes, you'd better, I can't think of anything else.'

'*Me!*' he yelled.

'Oh, Nicky!' She hugged him. 'You are a funny boy.'
They began to laugh. 'Right, my turn again.'

It helped her to forget, not to hurt so much. It was
easier that way. She could hear voices, and sounds of
activity from the kitchen. She began to plan, while
Nicky looked around to guess her letter, where she
would go when she left. It wouldn't be Alison and
Nicky leaving, it would be Jan. She wouldn't go back
to London, because she didn't want to. She would go
somewhere far away, and get a job, earn a living; it
didn't matter what the job was, she would be free and
independent for the first time in her life. But she would
make sure she didn't fall in love again.

It would be soon now, because Alison was nearly well
enough, and the house next door, the one they had
made such plans about, would soon be completed. Jan
had transferred money from her London bank to the
one in the village nearby. She was financially independent, at the very least for several months, and it
would give her time to look around. She might even do
what she had always wanted to do, but never been able
to, tour England at a leisurely pace in her car. She had
never been able to because her mother had thought the
idea ridiculous and totally unfitting for a young woman

in her position. She was free of her mother now, free emotionally. That at least Sandor had done for her. I'm tougher than I realised, she thought, as she lay beside the sleeping man that night, and stared, wide awake, at the ceiling on which flecks of moonlight danced. I'm free of my mother. Perhaps, soon, I'll be free of him. I'll never forget him—how could I?—but he's helped me to grow up.

There was a farm in the Lake District where she had spent a brief, happy holiday with her mother and father as a child, before they were wealthy. She remembered it well, and wondered if it would still be run as a guest house. There was only one way to find out. But not yet. Not quite. When Alison was fully well, then. . . .

Jan eventually fell asleep. Her aunt's bed was a huge one, and if she was careful she didn't have to touch Sandor. Not that it seemed to matter. He kept very much to his own part, never reaching out, never near— not since Alison had arrived.

When she woke in the morning he had gone. She heard voices from the kitchen, the smell of bacon and toast drifted upwards, and she thought, still half asleep, tomorrow, tomorrow I'll go to the bank. It was Sunday, and the sound of the church bells woke her fully; she remembered, and wept. She had been married for two weeks. She got out of bed and began to look through her clothes, selecting those she would take. There were some blouses and dresses waiting to be ironed, and her suitcases were in the spare bedroom. It would be simple enough to partially pack today and leave the cases where they were. And in the morning draw the money from the bank, and wait. She heard sudden laughter, both of them laughing at something Nicky had shouted, and that was the moment she knew the truth. It was going to be tomorrow. Alison had Sandor to care for her now. They were a unit, the three of them, and she had no place there.

Very quietly she gathered up a drawerful of clean underwear and crept into the spare bedroom. Then she had a good wash, dressed, and went downstairs. Alison greeted her.

'I was going to bring your breakfast up,' she said. 'Or rather, Nicky and I were. How's your hand?'

'Oh, fine. Mmm, that smells good.' Jan sat down, as Sandor reappeared with the dogs from the back garden.

'It is a beautiful day,' he said. 'Shall we all go out for a ride later?'

Nicky jumped up and down. 'Yes, yes!' he shouted. 'Please!'

Jan began to eat. She wasn't going to go, but she wouldn't tell them until they were ready. She could get on with her ironing then, and her packing.

'That sounds nice,' said Alison.

'Then it is decided. Jan?'

She looked up. 'Of course. Very nice.' She smiled. It was getting easier for her to smile now. It hid an aching heart, but they would never know that. She had one more night here, though they didn't know that either, and she wondered if Sandor would care, even if he knew.

Later, as they washed and dried the breakfast dishes, and Sandor had gone out with Nicky to take the dogs for a walk, Alison, who had been rather quiet since breakfast, asked: 'Is everything all right, Jan?'

Jan nearly dropped the saucer she was drying. 'With me? Yes, fine.' She looked at Alison, to surprise a look of concern mingled with something else she didn't understand. Pity? She didn't want that. She laughed. 'I'm fine,' she repeated, and Alison turned away, biting her lip. What was it? Jan had caught a glimpse of something similar on the other girl's face before, and it had always been her cue to put a wall of reserve round herself. Her heart started to bump. She felt terribly insecure, shut out, and she didn't like it.

'Only I——' Alison began, as if steeling herself to say something difficult. 'I feel—guilty.'

'What about?' Jan couldn't keep the brittle tension from her voice. 'Why should you feel guilty? I offered to look after you, and Nicky is very good——'

'It's not that,' said Alison miserably. 'It's something else, only I don't know how to tell you. Only Sandor said——'

Jan thought she would choke. 'I don't want to know,' she said quietly. 'Honestly, I'd rather not——' Leave me alone, she wanted to cry. Can't you see how unhappy I am?

'But I can't go on living a lie,' Alison burst out. 'I must tell you——'

The door opened and Sandor came in, carrying Nicky, who was crying. Alison rushed to him, half turning as if to appeal to Jan, a brief glimpse of something desperate in her eyes. Then the moment was lost.

Nicky had fallen and grazed his knee. His dignity was more hurt than his person, but he was gradually soothed at the fuss being made over him. So the moment passed, and was gone for good. But Jan thought she knew what Alison had been going to say. When she found out how wrong she was, it was nearly too late.

CHAPTER TEN

JAN waited until they were almost on the point of departure for their outing, then said: 'I've got a fearful headache—I'm awfully sorry, but would you mind if I didn't come?' She knew she looked as though she had. Since the strange conversation with Alison, she had felt gradually more drained, and it was only partly a lie.

Alison looked at Sandor quickly. Jan caught the look, and it seemed to set the seal on her doubts and fears. He said, very quietly:

'Then we won't go, of course.'

'But you must!' She rubbed her forehead. 'I'll be fine. I just need to be quiet for a while, that's all. And you can't disappoint Nicky. Please—go.'

'Are you sure?' Alison looked as though she would like to wring her hands. Her pretty face was clouded.

'Quite sure.' Jan even managed a smile. 'Off you go. Will you be having tea out?'

'Yes. And you will rest?' Sandor asked.

'I will.' It was easier now to look at him and see only a stranger. She didn't really know him, she never had. She never would. Better that way. 'I'll probably sit outside in the garden for a while, it's such a glorious day.' She patted Nicky's head. 'Tell me all about it when you get back, won't you?'

Ten minutes later she waved them off, went back into the house and switched on the iron.

When they returned, soon after seven, her two suitcases were packed and locked up in the boot of her car, her cheque book was ready in her handbag, and the letter to Sandor was with it. In the morning, before she left the cottage, she was going to put it on the cupboard at his side of the bed for him to find that evening after work. By which time she would be a few hundred miles away.

She had the television already on when they came in; she intended to watch it all evening. She didn't want to talk to either Sandor or Alison, in case she gave herself away. She felt wretched and miserable, and tried to snap herself out of it because the days of self-pity were over—but when Sandor asked if anyone wanted a drink she decided she might as well. It would help her to sleep, and she needed rest for the long, long drive ahead. The journey from her marriage. 'I'll have gin and tonic, please,' she said.

'Nothing for me, thanks,' said Alison. 'I'm going to have an early night. I enjoyed the ride out very much and the fresh sea air has tired me.'

Sandor poured gin and tonic for them both. Shortly afterwards, Alison said goodnight and went up to bed, and when Sandor went to take the dogs out Jan recklessly downed two nearly neat gins. She felt almost immediately delightfully tiddly, and much, much better.

It was her last night, and she felt reckless, and she didn't care. When Sandor said he was going to bed she looked at him. 'I'm going to have a bath,' she said.

'Fine.' He looked at her briefly, and she smiled to herself. She would make her last night something for him to remember. The room spun round gently as she left it and climbed the stairs to the bathroom. She wasn't running away, she was doing something entirely unselfish for probably the first time in her life, but before she made the grand, noble gesture to end all gestures, she was going to make sure that Sandor remembered her as a woman. It was not much to ask. Alison would have him to herself from tomorrow onwards. . . .

She soaked in a hot foam bath, dried herself, then took her special scented body lotion from her toilet bag. It was rich, with a musky erotic perfume that lingered, and Sandor had already told her, in secret whispers on their wedding night, what it did to him. She smiled a little smile to herself, wrapped the towel round her naked body, and making sure she was walking steadily, went into the bedroom.

Sandor was reading a very heavy book in bed. He looked up when Jan went in. He said nothing, merely looked at her.

'I want to put my body lotion on,' said Jan, 'only it's difficult with my cut finger. I'm awfully sorry to trouble you, but would you——' she hesitated delicately, disguising an intrusive hiccup by turning it into a cough, and walked slowly forward, letting the towel drop as she handed him the plastic bottle.

She heard his indrawn breath, saw his eyes darken, then he said: 'Turn round.' Obediently she did so, hiding a smile. She heard him uncap the bottle, then his hand, cool on her back, smoothing in the pink creamy lotion. Across her back, very steadily, then on her shoulders, and she arched her body, then leaned slightly sideways.

'Mmm, that's it,' she said. 'I can't reach there at the best of times.' Her voice was husky. She had started something off deliberately, almost coldbloodedly, but it was having an effect on her, too. 'Can I sit down?' she murmured. 'That gin——' She went and sat on the bed and he sat beside her, and now that her back was finished he began to run the lotion on her neck at the front and she leaned her head back, and said: 'Ah, that's nice, just down a little——' Only then, suddenly, it was both his hands, and no lotion on them, just him. She murmured: 'But there's no——' before he pushed her back on to the bed, very gently, and his hands were doing wonderful things that had nothing to do with applying lotion. She gave a little sigh and said. 'If you're not going to put lotion on me perhaps I'd better put some on you,' and began to unbutton his pyjama jacket. But she didn't have time to finish that because his body was closer, closer, too close for safety, and his lips came down on hers. The lips of a man who is hungry and is not prepared to wait any longer. Jan slid her arms round his hard muscular body and gave herself up to the sheer physical excitement of him, then there was no more time for words, only the wonder, and desire that needed no words to be expressed. . . .

She awoke, and it was nearly morning, the early sun growing brighter outside by the minute, Jan looked at Sandor, to remember him, and what had been. She felt no guilt at having stolen him from Alison for one night. It was her last time. Soon she would leave, and it would all be over. At the memory of his lovemaking, hours before, she went warm, and felt a surge of love for him that was so overwhelming that she nearly cried out. He opened his eyes drowsily, as if perhaps he had heard the unspoken sound, and looked along the pillow at her. She felt his slight movement, then his hand was upon her body, on her breasts, her stomach, her hips; he slid closer, and she knew the warmth of him and the desire that was once more in him, for her. She lifted herself slightly and moved into the shelter and protection of his arms. He made love to her with a kind of sad sweetness, a gentleness that once more surprised her. He could be so different each time, as if he possessed many moods. And this, now, was the most wonderful, long, dizzying spiral of delight and ecstasy that she had ever known.

He left her still half asleep, and she turned over in bed to relive it again and fell asleep, thinking his name, seeing his face, knowing how much she loved him, and always would.

Alison was in the kitchen preparing a drink of warm milk for Nicky when she left. Jan wanted to say good-bye, but could not. She had hugged Nicky, secretly, in the lounge, where he was engrossed in a schools programme on television, she had checked that the letter to Sandor was on the bedside table, and she had stuffed her toilet bag inside a shopping bag. It stood by the front door.

'I'm going to the bank in Medford,' she told Alison, 'then I'll do some shopping.'

'Will you be in for lunch?'

Jan hesitated only briefly. 'Er—no, I'll eat out. You're all right?'

'I'm fine,' Alison smiled. 'Thanks to your looking after me.'

It was time to go, before Alison began again about things which were better left unspoken. 'Well, I'm off. Goodbye.' Jan smiled at Alison, and her heart was heavy, but the girl would understand, when she read the note Jan had enclosed in Sandor's letter. She went out of the house without a backward glance and ran to her car. She was suddenly frightened that Sandor might appear and call her back, ask her why she was leaving. She felt like a criminal on the run. Suppose he had just come back to the cottage for something, gone upstairs, seen the note—was even now running down——

She switched on the engine and drove away, and when she passed the house he was building she kept her eyes firmly on the road ahead. That was not her house; it never would be. Whatever his future life it would not be with Jan. She hoped it would be with Alison, particularly for Nicky, and the unborn baby's sake. Perhaps I have done some good after all, she thought. Indirectly. This could have brought them together.

The thoughts passed through her mind as she drove to the bank, accompanied by pictures that were more disturbing. Images of Sandor, loving, as he had been at first. Even his face when they had first met, the hard aggressive-seeming man resenting her intrusion. The sparks had flown, and it had been the beginning of— what? Not love, she knew that now, not on his part anyway. Infatuation, a strong physical attraction—yes, those, but not love. It had been a brief encounter, one she would never forget.

The bank manager was helpful, hiding his undoubted surprise at Jan's drawing out nearly a thousand pounds from her account. She explained that she would be visiting the Lake District, and asked him to give her a note for the bank manager at the Kendal branch of her bank in case she needed any more transferred. This was accomplished at a leisurely pace, she thanked him and departed, after buying some food from the grocer's across the road from the bank.

Then she was on her way. As the miles rolled past, so did her heart ease. Perhaps, when she was well away, the pain would go. Perhaps. . . .

She stopped for food at a motorway restaurant midafternoon, drove on until, late in the evening, she reached Lancaster. There was no point in going on to try and find the farm in the dark, the morning would be better. Jan found a hotel not too far from the motorway and booked in under the name of Hunter, and there she watched television with several elderly people in the lounge until it was time to go to bed. She was aware that some of the guests watched her curiously, a young woman travelling alone, but with usual British reserve no one asked her any questions, save the politest ones, commenting on the beautiful weather, and had she travelled far that day? She had tea and biscuits with a Colonel Lapham and his wife at suppertime, and was treated to a long and slightly boring account of his life in India, to which she listened with polite attention. It helped her to forget. It was also a good soporific, and when at last she bade them goodnight, it was to go up to her room and fall into a deep dreamless sleep.

She breakfasted early and set off on the final stage of her journey, to find the farm of happy memories, a few miles outside Kendal. If it wasn't still a guest house, she would find somewhere else. And she would find a job, perhaps not immediately, but certainly after a week or so.

She needed her map now. The minor roads were confusing, after all those years, and several times she had to stop and ask locals if they knew where High Hill Farm was. The glorious Lakeland trees and mountains were misty in the heat, promising a beautiful day to come, and cars from all countries passed her, tourist-crowded, everyone having a good time, cameras at the ready. People picnicked by the roadsides, on the grass verges, and Jan passed a Rolls-Royce in a layby, and a family having lunch on small collapsible tables, being served champagne by a grey-uniformed chauffeur. She nearly laughed out loud at that. Only in England, she thought. No wonder the Dutch and the Germans and the Americans come over here every year! It's for scenes like that, priceless. Her mood was lifting. There was the summer ahead, and when it was over and autumn came, then she would have to decide what to do next. But there was time, and the wounds would heal, and she would be stronger mentally. She might even go back to London.

She saw the farmhouse ahead of her; the sign she sought was still there, weatherbeaten, a little battered after so many years, but saying what she had hoped: 'High Hill Farm. Accommodation. B. & B. and Evening Meals. Props. Mr and Mrs J. H. Cowan.'

They would be older, but it was the same couple. They wouldn't remember her, and that didn't matter, in fact it was better, but they had always been kind, full of humour, a hard-working couple born and bred in the Lake District with children, undoubtedly now grown up themselves and almost certainly married.

Jan drove up the steep wide path to the front door and switched off the engine. She felt as if she were coming home. She got out and pressed the front door bell, and waited.

'Well now,' said Mrs Cowan, her round rosy-cheeked face beaming at Jan. 'We're crowded out, me dear, I must be honest—I do wish you'd phoned. 'Twould have saved you all this trouble finding us.' She passed Jan a plate of shortbread, and added more tea to her own cup. They were sitting in the large overcrowded family living room, and a dog and cat wandered in, inspecting Jan and then going out, no doubt to report to their farm companions. Jan's heart sank.

'I'm sorry about that,' she said. 'Of course I should have written or phoned, but I came up on the spur of the moment.'

'I'd try and squeeze you in—your face looks familiar, me dear. It's puzzling me—but we're a bit short of help to be honest. My youngest daughter was helping us, but two days ago she was taken ill with her appendix—she's fine now, but—well, she'll need a bit of coddling for a week or so——'

'Do you want help?'

Mrs Cowan looked mildly surprised. 'Are you offering, me dear? It's well nigh impossible to get staff at this time of year—but you're here on holiday!'

It was time to explain. It was time, because Jan sensed the genuine openness of this kindly woman, and also knew what she wanted to do. 'I stayed here years ago with my mother and father,' she said. 'And I've always remembered your farm with great affection. I had to get away from a—bad—emotional situation——' she hesitated, 'and—I decided to see if you could put me up for a while until I found a job. If you want me—and I promise you I can work hard—I'd love to help you.'

Mrs Cowan slapped her knee. 'Well now, the answer to my prayers! Can you make beds and wait on at table—and wash up and tidy?'

'Yes.'

'You'll have to sleep in a tiny attic bedroom——'

'That sounds fine.'

Mrs Cowan looked at her very shrewdly, narrowing her eyes. 'I do recognise you, you know. Isn't your mother——' she paused as if not sure how to say it.

'Coral Hunter—the Zesty-Cola woman. You'd have known her as Mrs Ingles—that was my father's name. My late stepfather adopted me when they married.'

'There now! I was right. I've seen her photo many a time—and yours too. My, but you were just a little scrap when you stayed here. I remember I thought you needed feeding up—and now look at you, a beautiful young woman. Wait till Jim sees you—his eyes'll pop out!'

Jan laughed. She began to feel happy for the first time in days and days. 'Am I to take it I've passed the interview?' she said.

Mrs Cowan smiled warmly. 'You have. Let's have another cup of tea to celebrate. Then I'll show you your room and we'll discuss wages. Er—I can't pay a fortune, you understand——'

'I'd work for nothing!' said Jan.

'Oh, we don't expect that! Heavens, what a thought! But you'll be well fed, I promise you. We've two Swedish boys here, and a German couple with two children, and two Americans arrive later today from Scotland. I don't do lunches, but there's a big evening meal to prepare, and breakfast. Come on, me dear, I'll tell you when you've seen your room. And I'll find you an overall. If you feel like starting work today, I'd be very grateful.'

'I do. Thank you, Mrs Cowan, you're very kind.'

'Call me Daisy, dear, everyone else does. Right, let's go.'

The room was indeed tiny, with a sloping ceiling that you would bang your head on if you weren't careful, but it had a spectacular view from the window, and a comfortable-looking single bed. A chair and wardrobe were the only other items of furniture that the attic had space for, but it would suffice, and Jan turned to the farmer's wife, resisting the impulse to hug her.

'It's lovely,' she smiled.

'Hmm, t'would be a bit tiny for me,' Mrs Cowan patted her ample hips and chuckled, 'but you're a slim lass, you'll manage. There's a washbasin out on your landing, no space in here for it, but it's private 'cos only you'll come up here. Now you can get your luggage when you want. If you come down with me we'll go and tell Jim, and then you can get started.' She led the way out, and Jan followed.

It was being flung in at the deep end, but it was precisely what Jan needed. She served dinner that night to the two young Swedes, and the German family, and the two Americans who had arrived only minutes before seven-thirty. Mrs Cowan helped her, and it was a constant dash from kitchen to dining room with no time to talk or even to think of anything but what dish came next, and for whom.

When it was over, and the dining room was empty, Jan cleared away, feeling as if her feet would drop off.

Mrs Cowan was baking a batch of biscuits for supper and the following day, and the kitchen was filled with spicy aroma.

'Well, how did you manage?' Mrs Cowan asked, as Jan plunged her hands in the soapy water.

'My feet are aching, but apart from that I think I'll live,' Jan rejoined cheerfully.

Mrs Cowan laughed. 'You'll get over that in a day or two. It's a big help to me, believe me—you did very well indeed. Why, I'd have thought you'd been waiting on table for years!' She began drying the dishes with a speed born of years of practice. 'We'll have a cuppa in a minute, then set the tables for supper—they just have tea and home made biscuits, but bless 'em, these foreign visitors enjoy a touch of old England, and I for one am not going to let them down.'

'How late do they have it?' Jan had visions of staggering to bed at one. Would she live that long?

'Oh, never fear, I leave out thermos flasks of boiling water for them to do their own! I have to be up at five, love, and some of them come in at midnight.'

Jan sighed in relief. She was learning. 'What time would you like me up in the morning?'

'About seven-thirty. Breakfast for them is at eight-thirty to nine. After that you can Hoover and strip the Germans' beds. They're leaving tomorrow, and we've a party of French arriving. Clean round the bedrooms —then the afternoon you can have off till six. That's when I visit my daughter Caroline.'

Jan saw that she was going to have to revise her

mental time clock. It would be all go in the mornings, probably from seven-thirty till one or two, and then time off until dinner. So be it. She would soon adjust. In fact she was adjusting already. There was one minor remaining problem. 'Er—until I buy an alarm clock,' she said, 'would you give me a call in the morning? I've a feeling I'll be sleeping like a log, and I'd hate to let you down on my first morning.'

'I will do, love. I'll do more, I'll give you an alarm clock that would wake anybody—it's like a fire bell. You'll wake with *that*! Now, love, we'll have that cup of tea, then we can sit and talk for a while about your time off and your wages.'

At half past ten Jan was nearly asleep on her feet. Mrs Cowan, seeing this, suggested with a chuckle that it was time she went to bed, and Jan duly departed, clutching an old-fashioned alarm clock with a huge bell atop it, and feeling very grateful to the older woman.

She was asleep within seconds of her head touching the pillow.

The clangour of a thousand bells filled her ears. There was a fire, and Sandor was rushing in to rescue Nicky and Alison while Jan stood on a sloping lawn crying, praying he would save them—Jan sat up, frightened, heart thudding, to hear the alarm clock giving its all on the windowsill, vibrating so much that it was about to fall off. She grabbed it just in time, switched off the alarm, and calmed down instantly. It had been a dream. Mrs Cowan had been right about the alarm anyway. She was well and truly awake, and ready to face the day ahead.

By the time Mrs Cowan knocked on her door she was dressed and ready to go down. And so her day began.

After all her work was done, it was past one. She was free until six, and the knowledge was heady. Five hours to do just as she liked. Jan went up to her room for her bag and car keys, saw the bed, and decided to have a ten-minute lie-down before going out. She would go to Windermere and do some shopping, telephone her mother, in case she had been trying to contact her in the cottage, just to reassure her that she was all right, then come back in good time for dinner. She lay down, planning the rest of her day, and closed her eyes, just for a few minutes. . . .

When she woke the clock showed that it was just past five. Startled, unbelieving, she looked at her watch. There was no mistake; both showed the same time. She had slept for four hours. She crept guiltily downstairs and confessed what had happened to Mrs Cowan, who was preparing several chickens for the oven. The older woman thought it very amusing. 'Sit down, love,' she said, 'I've got the kettle on, won't take a minute to make tea. That'll wake you up.' She went on busily stuffing the chickens. 'Oh, I nearly forgot! There was a phone call for you—a lady. I thought you'd gone out walking or I'd have called you.'

'A lady? Did she give a name?' Jan was puzzled. Could it be her mother?

'No, love, just said she was a friend. Now, if it had been a man I'd have been more cautious, 'cos you—er—told me you'd had an emotional problem and in my experience that's always the fault of some fellow—it's all right, my dear, I'm not going to pry, but as I said, she sounded so nice I said you were here and she thanked me. Then the line went funny, so I shouted to her to ring you back later when you come in—then we were cut off.'

Jan looked at the older woman, her feelings confused. Nobody knew she was here. 'Can I make a pot of tea?' she asked quietly.

'It's not upset you, has it? She sounded very nice, really.'

'No, it's not that. It's just that no one knows where I am.'

Mrs Cowan frowned. 'That's odd. Tell you what, when she phones again I'll find out who she is before I let her speak to you. That's it, love, tea bags over there. I could do with a cup myself. Then I'll get these in the oven. It's all go, isn't it?' Her practical attitude was sufficient to shake Jan out of her doubts. It would turn out to be nothing, and there was work to be done.

But the mystery caller didn't ring again, and by bedtime Jan was so tired she had forgotten about it. She curled up with a good thriller that Jim Cowan had lent her from his vast store of paperbacks, read for half an hour before putting the light out and falling fast asleep.

The alarm woke her, but she was getting used to it,

and it wasn't accompanied by fire nightmares, it was just simply a very loud noise. She was downstairs dressed and ready for work at half past seven.

Breakfast was successfully dealt with, dishes washed and cleared, and Jan began helping Mrs Cowan with the housework. The radio accompanied their tasks. Mrs Cowan regaled her with several amusing stories about previous guests, and the morning passed quickly.

They were sitting down in the living room having a very welcome cup of coffee at noon when the front doorbell rang. Jan looked up. 'Shall I——' she began.

'No, love, it'll be someone wanting a room. I'll give them one or two addresses. You sit there and finish your coffee.' Mrs Cowan went out.

Minutes passed. Jan could hear faint voices, but the music from the radio effectively blurred any details. There was nothing to warn her, no premonition, nothing.

Until Mrs Cowan returned, and with a very odd expression on her face said: 'It's someone for you, love.'

Jan looked up, saw what was on the other's face, and felt faint. 'Who——' she began.

Mrs Cowan smiled, her features softening. 'It's a man. He says to tell you he loves you very much.'

Jan tried to stand up, and the room began to spin round. 'Please'—she said through dry lips—'please——' Mrs Cowan came forward and took her arm, and Sandor walked in the room.

CHAPTER ELEVEN

HE caught her as she fell, put her on the settee and knelt at her feet, his face white. Mrs Cowan, after one look at them both, picked up her coffee cup and vanished.

'Jan,' he said. 'Oh, Jan, what fools we've been!' He steadied her with his hands on her arms. 'Aren't you going to say anything—even if it's only, "go away"?'

'Where's Alison?' she whispered.

'With her husband and son at the cottage, looking after the dogs I had to leave to come chasing up here after you.'

'Her—husband?' Her teeth began to chatter, because this was surely a bad dream, and she went very cold.

'Yes. I sent for him when she was taken ill—I wanted him to arrive so that when you saw him, actually for yourself, you might believe what you certainly did not believe before.'

Jan shook her head, dazed. 'I don't—don't understand.'

'No, I'm quite sure you don't.' He sat beside her on the settee. 'But I'll go through it step by step, and then perhaps you will. And then perhaps also, we can forgive each other for all the time we have wasted and the unhappiness we have caused each other.' He put his arm round her and she didn't resist.

'I have been wrong. I should have told you about Alison and Nicky at the beginning, but I didn't, because, for me, it is difficult to talk about my family. I had a younger brother, Alexei, who was, to put it bluntly, a bit of a rake. I think your mother had heard some stories of the wrong brother when she said about all my women—but that is unimportant.

'Alexei was killed three years ago. Nicky is his child, not mine. Alison was very young when she met him, and fell in love—and the inevitable happened. I regret to say that Alexei's sense of responsibility was not as strong as mine. He paid maintenance for the baby, but that was all. When he died I made it my business to trace Alison, and give her a good sum each month for her and Nicky. She moved from London—her parents had been very harsh on her in my opinion—and I bought her a cottage in the village where you saw her. She pretended to be a young widow, naturally enough, and there met a young Merchant Navy seaman called Brian when he was on leave one time. They were married a year ago. The child she is expecting is his, not mine.'

'Why—why didn't you tell me?' She shivered.

'Because you had read the letter and immediately assumed the worst, possibly also remembering what your mother had said. That hurt me—oh yes, I am hard, but my love for you goes deep, and I was hurt. I was—forgive me—teaching you a lesson. Only you taught me one.' He closed his eyes. 'Dear God, when I read your letter, that you loved me and yet were willing to sacrifice that love for me and the woman you thought I loved, I realised just how stubborn and stupid I had been. I set about tracing where you had gone. You told Alison you were going to the bank— so I went there first and had a talk with the manager. He was very reluctant to tell me anything at first, but I persuaded him—frankly I bribed him by promising him my account. That did it! He told me about the letter to Kendal. I then phoned your mother, told her of our misunderstanding and asked her if she would have any idea where you might have gone. Believe me, I was prepared to hire a team of detectives to comb the Lake District for your car—but it was not necessary. Your mother suggested this farm as being a place where you had spent a happy holiday years ago. I asked Alison to phone, and she did.' He shrugged. 'Brian had arrived back by then, so yesterday afternoon I set off.'

'I'm working here,' Jan said in a small voice, because at that moment the complexity of what she had heard was almost too much to understand.

'I know. Your nice farmer's wife told me that. No problem. I shall stay with you, we shall have our honeymoon——'

'But——' Wide-eyed, she look at him. 'How can——'

'You have a bed? Good.'

'It's a single bed,' she said firmly, but a smile of pure happiness was beginning to break through.

'Better still.' Sandor kissed her. 'I like that.' Then he laughed.

'But—my work—I can't let her down——'

'You will not. I shall hire someone for her, even if I have to get a London agency to send someone. I shall go and speak with her now.'

Jan caught hold of his arm. 'Wait. Let me absorb all of this. It's all so sudden——'

'Yes, I know. But the main thing, the most important thing of all, remember, is this—I love you with all my heart. I always have and I always will.'

She remembered the one dreadful night when she had thought he was speaking Alison's name. But now she realised it had been Alexei. On such flimsy misunderstandings can lives be ruined. 'Oh, my darling Sandor,' she whispered, 'I love you too—very much. That's why I left. I thought—it was her—when I saw you talking, caught your glances—— Oh, I've been so stupid—and she tried to tell me one day, but I wouldn't listen. I was frightened of what I thought she was going to say.' She sighed, but it was of contentment, not anguish.

'I have more to say to you, much more, but somewhere very private. Let me go and talk to Mrs Cowan first, then I will bring my case up to our bedroom.' Sandor leaned over and whispered in her ear, and she found herself, to her dismay, going pink, like a schoolgirl on her first date.

Faintly she said: 'Yes, I've brought the lotion, but——'

He silenced her with a kiss, then: 'You'll see, very soon—you'll see.' He pulled her to her feet, and when he looked down at her the love shone in his eyes.

'Ah,' he said, 'I have found you. You will never escape me again. Never.' He slid his arms down her body. 'Go upstairs. I will follow.' His voice had gone very husky.

'I don't want to escape,' Jan whispered. 'Don't be long, my love. I want to begin our honeymoon.'

'Ah yes—then had you not better return your wedding ring to its rightful place?' He produced her ring, which she had left behind with her letter, from his pocket, and slid it on her finger.

'Now we are married again,' he whispered. 'Go—quickly, before I am tempted to make love to you here.'

He meant it too. Jan fled. She didn't want Mrs Cowan to be too shocked. She wondered if anyone else had ever had such an unusual start to a honeymoon. The other woman's laughter followed her up the stairs. It seemed she and Sandor were getting on famously—but Jan hoped he wouldn't stay too long talking.

She went into the tiny, cosy attic bedroom, drew the curtains, and waited impatiently for her husband, the man she would always love, more than life itself. Then she heard his footsteps on the stairs and opened the door wide.

Best Seller Romances

Accept 4
Best Selling Romances
Absolutely
FREE

Enjoy the very best of love, romance and intrigue brought to you by Mills & Boon. Every month Mills & Boon very carefully select 3 Romances that have been particularly popular in the past and re-issue them for the benefit of readers who may have missed them first time round. Become a subscriber and you can receive six superb novels every two months, and your personal membership card will entitle you to a whole range of special benefits too: a free newsletter, packed with exclusive book offers, recipes, competitions and your guide to the stars, plus there are other bargain offers and big cash savings.

**AND an Introductory FREE GIFT for YOU.
Turn over the page for details.**

As a special introduction we will send you
FOUR superb and exciting
Best Seller Romances – yours to keep Free
– when you complete and return
this coupon to us.

At the same time we will reserve a
subscription to Mills & Boon Bestseller
Romances for you. Every two months you
will receive the 6 specially selected
Bestseller novels delivered direct to your
door. Postage and packing is always
completely Free. There is no obligation or
commitment – you can cancel your
subscription at any time.

**You have absolutely nothing to lose and a whole world of
romance to gain.** Simply fill in and post the coupon today to:-
MILLS & BOON READER SERVICE, FREEPOST,
P.O. BOX 236, CROYDON, SURREY CR9 9EL.

Please note:- READERS IN SOUTH AFRICA write to
Mills & Boon Ltd., Postbag X3010,
Randburg 2125, S. Africa.

- -

FREE BOOKS CERTIFICATE

**To: Mills & Boon Reader Service, FREEPOST, P.O. Box 236,
Croydon, Surrey CR9 9EL.**

Please send me, free and without obligation, four Mills & Boon Bestseller Romances, and reserve a Reader Service Subscription for me. If I decide to subscribe I shall receive, following my
free parcel of books, six new Bestseller Romances every two months for £6.00 , post and packing free. If I decide not to subscribe, I shall write to you within 10 days. The free books are mine
to keep in any case. I understand that I may cancel my subscription at any time simply by writing
to you. I am over 18 years of age.
Please write in BLOCK CAPITALS.

Name _____

Address _____

_____

_____Postcode_____

SEND NO MONEY — TAKE NO RISKS.

*Remember, postcodes speed delivery. Offer applies in UK only and is not valid to present subscribers
Mills & Boon reserve the right to exercise discretion in granting membership. If price
changes are necessary you will be notified. Offer expires 31st December 1985.*

4BS

EP1